I0610273

Ely Hargrove

Anecdotes of Archery

Ely Hargrove

Anecdotes of Archery

ISBN/EAN: 9783337367190

Printed in Europe, USA, Canada, Australia, Japan

Cover: Foto ©Andreas Hilbeck / pixelio.de

More available books at **www.hansebooks.com**

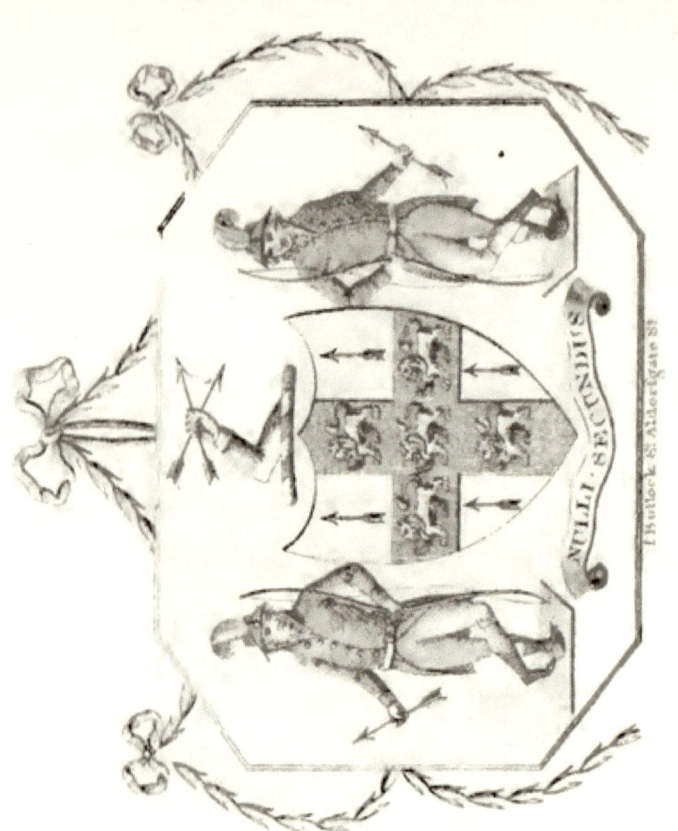

NULLI SECUNDUS

J. Bullock, 61 Aldersgate St.

Anecdotes

OF

ARCHERY;

FROM THE

Earliest Ages to the Year 1791.

Including an ACCOUNT of

The MOST FAMOUS ARCHERS

OF ANCIENT AND MODERN TIMES;

With some curious Particulars in the LIFE of

ROBERT FITZ-OOTH EARL OF HUNTINGTON,

Vulgarly called

ROBIN HOOD.

THE PRESENT STATE OF ARCHERY,

WITH

THE DIFFERENT SOCIETIES IN GREAT BRITAIN,

Particularly those of

Yorkshire, Lancashire, and Durham.

BY E. HARGROVE.

YORK:

Printed for E. HARGROVE, Bookseller, Knaresbro';
And sold by all the Booksellers of York, Leeds, and Ripon.
M,DCC,XCII.

TO

GEORGE ALLAN, Esq. F. A. S.

IN GRATITUDE

FOR MANY FAVOURS RECEIVED,

THESE

ANECDOTES OF ARCHERY

ARE MOST HUMBLY

INSCRIBED

BY THE

AUTHOR

THE Bow is the moſt ancient, and hath been the moſt univerſal, of all weapons; and probably was uſed againſt the beaſts of the foreſts, long before men made war upon each other:—We find it uſed by the moſt powerful and civilized, as well as the moſt barbarous and uncultivated, nations. In Holy Writ* we are told ISAAC called his ſon ESAU, and ſaid, " Now therefore take, I " pray thee, thy weapons, thy quiver and thy bow, " and go out to the field, and take me ſome ve- " niſon; and make me ſavory meat, ſuch as I " love, and bring it to me, that I may eat, that " my ſoul may bleſs thee before I die."

JONATHAN, the ſon of SAUL, was a ſkilful Archer; but it ſeems this weapon had been neglected amongſt the armies of Iſrael, for in the fatal battle near mount Gilboa, betwixt SAUL and the Philiſtines, we are told †. " The battle " went ſore againſt Saul; and the Archers hit him; " and he was ſore wounded of the Archers."

* Gen. xxvii. 3. † 1 Samuel, xxxi. 3.

A 3

In the next chapter we are told, that DAVID gave orders for the children of Judah, to be taught the use of the bow.

= ⌀ =

In the Iliad, we find the bow sometimes mentioned, though it does not seem to have been of general use in either army during that memorable war. The poet speaking of PARIS, and describing the dress and arms of that delicate warrior *, says——

. . . . The panther's speckled hide
Flow'd o'er his armour with an easy pride;
His bended bow across his shoulders flung,
His sword beside him negligently hung;
Two pointed spears he shook, with gallant grace,
And dar'd the bravest of the Grecian race †.

PANDARUS aiming an arrow at MENELAUS, the action is thus described ‡ :

Now with full force the yielding horn he bends,
Drawn to an arch, and joins the doubling ends;
Close to the breast he strains the nerve below,
Till the barb'd point approach the circling bow :
Th' impatient weapon whizzes on the wing,
Sounds the tough horn, and twangs the quiv'ring string.

* And yet this was the man who afterwards insidiously slew the great Achilles, by wounding him in the heel with an arrow, when he was going to marry Polyxena, in the temple of Apollo.
† Iliad, Book III. line 27.
‡ Iliad, Book IV. line 152.

The Locrians were a body of troops in the Grecian army, who occasionally ufed both the bow and the fling *.

The Locrian fquadrons nor the jav'lin wield,
Nor bear the helm, nor lift the moony fhield;
But fkill'd from far the flying fhaft to wing,
Or whirl the founding pebble from the fling.
Dextrous with thefe they aim a certain wound,
Or fell the diftant warrior to the ground.
Thus in the van, the Telamonian train
Throng'd in bright arms, a preffing fight maintain:
For in the rear the Locrian Archers lie,
Whofe ftones and arrows intercept the fky;
The mingled tempeft on the foes they pour;
Troy's fcatt'ring orders open to the fhow'r.

The fuitors of Penelope, having in vain at-tempted to bend the bow of Ulysses, (that hero being prefent, difguifed like a beggar) he with much difficulty obtains leave to try his fkill †.

. . . . One hand aloft difplay'd
The bending horns, and one the ftring effay'd.
From his effaying hand the ftring let fly,
Twang'd fhort and fharp, like the fhrill fwallow's cry.
A general horror ran thro' all the race,
Sunk was each heart, and pale was every face:
Then fierce the hero o'er the threfhold ftrode;
Stript of his rags, he blaz'd out like a god.

* Iliad, Book XIII. line 891.
† Odyffey, Book XXI. line 446.

Full in their face the lifted bow he bore,
And quiver'd deaths, a formidable store;
Before his feet the rattling show'r he threw,
And thus terrific to the suitor crew:
" One vent'rous game this hand has won to-day,
Another, princes! yet remains to play;
Another mark our arrow must attain,
PHŒBUS! assist;—nor be the labour vain."
Swift as the word the parting arrow sings,
And bears thy fate, ANTINOUS, on its wings:
Wretch that he was, of unprophetic soul!
High in his hands he rear'd the golden bowl!
Even then to drain it, lengthen'd out his breath,
Chang'd to the deep, the bitter draught of death:
For fate, who fear'd, amidst a fearful band?
And fate to numbers, by a single hand?
Full thro' his throat ULYSSES' weapon past,
And pierc'd the neck: He falls and breaths his last.

ENEAS in celebrating the anniversary of his
father's funeral, amongst other sports and exercises, introduces Archery.

Forthwith ENEAS to the sports invites
All who with feather'd shafts wou'd try their skill,
And names the prizes.   With his ample hand
He from SERESTUS' ship a mast erects;
And on it by a rope suspended ties
A swift-wing'd dove, at which they all should aim
Their arrows: They assemble; and the lots
Shuffled into a brazen casque are thrown.
With fav'ring shouts HIPPOCOON first appears,
Offspring of HYRTACUS: Then MNESTHEUS next,
So lately victor in the naval strife,
And crown'd with olive-greens: EURYTION third,

Brother to thee, O PANDARUS! renown'd,
Who once, commanded to diffolve the league,
Didſt firſt among the Grecians hurl a dart:
ACESTES to the helmet's bottom ſinks/
The laſt; himſelf preſuming to attempt
The ſports of youth.   Then all with manly ſtrength
Bend their tough yeugh; each with his utmoſt force
All from their quivers draw their ſhafts: and firſt
Shot from the twanging nerve HIPPOCOON's flies
Along the ſky, beats the thin liquid air,
And on the body of the maſt adverſe
Stands fix'd: The maſt and frighted bird at once
Tremble, and all the cirque with ſhouts reſounds.
Next eager MNESTHEUS with his bended bow
Stands ready, and his eyes and arrow aim'd
Directs to heav'n; yet cou'd not reach the dove
Herſelf unfortunate, but cut the knots
And hempen ligaments in which ſhe hung
Ty'd by the feet upon the lofty maſt;
She flies into the winds and duſky clouds.
EURYTION then impatient, and long ſince
Holding his ready bow and fitted ſhaft,
Invokes his broth r; and, in open air,
Seeing the dove now ſhake her ſounding wings,
Transfixes her amidſt the clouds: The bird
Falls dead, and leaves her life among the ſtars.

———— ❦ ————

CYAXARES, king of the Medes, and great
grandfather to CYRUS, engaged ſome Scythian
Archers to teach his ſon the uſe of the bow.
This nation had a law, that their children ſhould
learn three things particularly, from the age of
five to that of twenty, viz. To ride a horſe well,

to fhoot well, and never to tell a lie. ZENO-
PHON obferves, that CYRUS was from a child
brought up to Archery.

═ ✧ ═

HERODOTUS informs us, that when CAMBYSES
had conquered EGYPT, and had thoughts of invading ÆTHIOPIA, he fent fome fpies before
him ; who, under pretence of carrying prefents
to the king, might privately inquire into the
ftrength and condition of the kingdom.   When
they were arrived at court, and had made their
prefents, the king of ÆTHIOPIA faid to them,
" It was not from any confideration of my friend-
" fhip, that the king of PERSIA fent you to me
" with thefe prefents; neither have you fpoken
" the truth, but are come into my kingdom as
" fpies.   If CAMBYSES was an honeft man he
" would defire no more than his own; and not
" endeavour to reduce a people under fervitude,
" who have never done him any injury.   How-
" ever, give him this bow from me, and let him
" know, that the king of ÆTHIOPIA advifes
" the king of PERSIA, to make war againft the
" ÆTHIOPIANS, when the PERSIANS fhall be
" able thus eafily to draw fo ftrong a bow ; and
" in the meanwhile to thank the gods, that they
" never infpired the ÆTHIOPIANS with a defire
" of extending their dominions beyond their own
" country."   Saying this, he unbent the bow,
and delivered it to the ambaffadors.

The prophets ISAIAH and JEREMIAH, both speak of this nation, as being famous for bending and handling the bow *.

The beft part of the armies of ALEXANDER the GREAT were Archers.

≈◡≈

THE bowmen of Athens performed wonders in many battles; but particularly under DE-MOSTHENES, their renowned general, when they defeated the Lacedemonians near the city of Pylos.   PLATO mentions, that one thoufand Archers were appointed for the ftanding guard of the city of Athens.   This celebrated philofopher was an advocate for Archery, and recommended to the Athenians that proper mafters might be employed by the ftate, to teach their youth the ufe of the bow; and that a large field fhould be fet apart, near every town and city, for that pur-pofe.

≈◡≈

THE Cretans began to teach their youth the ufe of the bow at feven years of age; and fo ex-pert were this people in the ufe of the weapon, that all the neighbouring monarchs were defirous of having a band of Cretan Archers in their armies. " The arrows of Gortynia," fays

* Ifaiah lxvi. 19.—Jeremiah xlvi. 9.

CLAUDIAN, " aimed from a trufty bow, are
" fure to wound, nor ever mifs the deftined
" mark."

═ ∽ ═

THE victories obtained by the Parthians, over
the Romans, was chiefly afcribed to their fuperiority in the ufe of their bows. With thefe they
purfued MARCUS ANTONINUS over the hills of
Media and Armenia,—conquered the noble Va-
lerian,—and flew the Apoftate Julian.

Though we find very little mention of the bow
in the Roman armies, yet they often employed
auxiliary Archers in their wars. DOMITIAN,
COMMODUS, and THEODOSIUS were accounted
excellent fhooters. It is evident alfo they had
mafters at Rome to teach the art, among whom
was T FLAVIUS EXPEDITUS; whofe image
SPON has given from a fepulchral bafs relief,
where he is called DOCTOR SAGITTARUM.

═ ∽ ═

LEO ordained that all the youth of Rome
fhould be compelled to ufe fhooting, more or lefs;
and always bear their bow and quiver about with
them, till they were eleven years old. He alfo
adds, " We ftrictly command you to make pro-
" clamation to all men under our dominion, which
" be either in war or peace; to all cities and
" towns; and, finally, to all manner of men,—
" that every free man have bow and arrows of

" his own, and every houfe have a bow and forty
" arrows for every occafion ; and that they exer-
" cife themfelves in holts, hills, dales, woods,
" and plains, to inure them to all the chances of
" war."

=== ⌀ ===

THE Artillery Company of London *, tho' they
have long difufed the **weapon,** are the remains of
the Ancient Fraternity **of Bowmen, or Archers.**
Artillery (*artillerie*) is a **French term,** fignifying
Archery : As the *King's Bowyer* is, in that lan-
guage, ftyled *Artillier du Roy*.

William the Conqueror had a confiderable number of bowmen in his **army at** the battle of Ha-
ftings : The names of the officers of this part of
his army is contained in the roll of Battle-Abbey † ;
they **are** in number feventy-three, and came from
the Vale of Rueil Bretviel, and **many** other places.
Amongft thefe we find the names of DUGLOSSE,
MOWBRAY, MORTIMER, HARECOURT, DEV-
REUX, ALLAN COUNT DE BRITAIGNE, &c.

As **this** victory was certainly obtained by the
help of the long-bow and broad-arrow ‡ ; fo it
was by **the** fame weapons that **the** Englifh afterwards **conquered** France.

* Archæologiæ, **vol. vii.**
† Fuller's Church Hiftory.
‡ Harold himfelf was flain by an arrow.

B

It may not be improper to infert in this place an excellent and curious comparifon between this weapon and our fire arms, mentioned in the life of WILLIAM the NORMAN by JOHN HAYWARD.

" One circumftance more I hold fit to be ob-
" ferved, that this victory was gotten only by
" means of the arrow; the ufe whereof was
" brought into this land afterwards. The Englifh
" being trained to the fight, did thereby chiefly
" maintain themfelves with honourable advantage
" againft all nations with whom they did contend
" in arms, being generally reputed the beft fhot in
" the world.   But of late years it hath been alto-
" gether laid afide; and inftead thereof, the
" harquebufs and calliver are brought into ufe, yet
" not without contradiction of many expert men
" of arms; who, albeit they do not reject the ufe
" of the fmall pieces, yet do they prefer the bow
" before them: Firft, for that, in a reafonable
" diftance, it is of greater certainty and force:
" Secondly, for that it difcharges fafter: Thirdly,
" for that more men may difcharge therewith at
" once; for only the firft rank difchargeth the
" piece, neither hurt they any but thofe that are
" in front; but with the bow ten or twelve ranks
" may difcharge together, and will annoy fo many
" ranks of the enemy: Laftly, for that the arrow
" doth ftrike more parts of the body; for in that it
" turneth by defcent, and not only point-blank,
" like the bullet, there is no part of the body but

" it may ſtrike, from tlle crown of the head, to
" the nailing of the foot to the ground. Here-
" upon it followeth, that the arrows falling ſo
" thick as hail upon the bodies of men, as leſs
" fearful of their fleſh, ſo much ſlenderly armed
" than in former times, muſt neceſſarily work
" more dangerous effects. Beſides theſe general
" reſpects, in many particular ſervices and times
" the uſe of the bow is of great advantage; if
" ſome defence lie before the enemy, the arrow
" may ſtrike where the bullet cannot; foul wea-
" ther may much hinder the diſcharge of the
" piece, but is of no great impediment to the diſ-
" charge of the bow: A horſe ſtruck with a bul-
" let, if the wound be not mortal, may perform
" good ſervice; but if an arrow be faſtened in
" his fleſh, the continual ſtirring thereof, occa-
" ſioned by the motion of himſelf, will force him
" to caſt of all command, and either beat down,
" or diſorder thoſe that are near. But the crack
" of the piece, ſome men ſay, doth ſtrike a terror
" in the enemy: True, if they be ſuch as never
" heard the like noiſe before; but a little uſe will
" extinguiſh theſe terrors. To men, yea to
" beaſts, acquainted with theſe cracks, they work
" a weak impreſſion of fear: And if it be true,
" which all men of action do hold, that the eye in
" all battles is firſt overcome, then againſt men
" equally accuſtomed to both, the ſight of the ar-
" row is more available to victory than the crack of
" the piece. Aſſuredly the duke, before the bat-

B 2

" tle, encouraged his men, for that they should
" deal with enemies who had no fhot. But I will
" leave this point to be determined by more dif-
" cerning judgment *."

WILLIAM himfelf was an admirable Archer,
and was fo ftrong, that few but himfelf could
bend the bow he ufed.

═ ◈ ═

WILLIAM II. being hunting in the New-Fo-
reft, in company with Sir WALTER TYRRELL,
and others; this knight unfortunately let fly an
arrow at a ftag, which glancing againft a tree,
took a different direction, and pierced the king's
breaft, who immediately expired. To perpetuate
the memory of fo remarkable an event, JOHN
LORD DELWAR, who had feen the tree grow-
ing, erected a pillar in the very place where it
ftood, with the following infcription :

" HERE STOOD THE OAK TREE ON WHICH
" AN ARROW, SHOT BY SIR WALTER TYR-
" RELL AT A STAG, GLANCED, AND STRUCK
" KING WILLIAM THE SECOND, SURNAMED
" RUFUS, IN THE BREAST, OF WHICH HE IN-
" STANTLY DIED, ON THE SECOND DAY OF
" AUGUST, A. D. 1100."

" KING WILLIAM THE SECOND, SURNA-
" MED RUFUS, BEING SLAIN AS BEFORE RE-

* See Harl. Mifcell. vol. ii.

" LATED, WAS LAID IN A CART BELONG-
" ING TO ONE PURKESS, AND DRAWN FROM
" THENCE TO WINCHESTER, AND BURIED
" IN THE CATHEDRAL CHURCH OF THAT
" CITY."

RICHARD STRONGBOW, Earl of Clare, Pem-
broke, and Buckingham, was famous for his
ftrength and fkill in Archery; after reducing Ire-
land for king Henry II. he died 1177.

RICHARD I. King of England, when be-
fieging the caftle of Chaluze, approached too near
the walls, and was killed by an arrow from a crofs-
bow, on the 8th of March 1199.

During the reign of this monarch we firft find
mention made of ROBIN HOOD *, who hath been
fo long celebrated as the chief of Englifh Archers.

The inteftine troubles of England were very
great at that time, and the country every where
infefted with outlaws and banditti; amongft whom
none were fo famous as this Sylvan hero and his
followers, whom STOW, in his Annals, ftyles
RENOWNED THIEVES. The perfonal courage of
this celebrated outlaw, his fkill in Archery, his
humanity, and efpecially his levelling principle, of

* Vide Rapin.

B 3

taking from the rich and giving to the poor, have ever fince rendered him the favourite of the common people.

SIR EDWARD COKE, in his Third Inftitute, page 197, fpeaks of Robin Hood, and fays, that men of his lawlefs profeffion were from him called *Roberdfmen*: He fays, that this notable thief gave not only a name to thefe kind of men, but mentions a Bay on the Yorkfhire coaft, called *Robin Hood's Bay*. He farther adds, that the Statute of Winchefter, 13th of Edward I. and another Statute of the 5th of Edward III. were made for the punifhment of Roberdfmen, and other felons.

Who was the author of the collection, called *Robin Hood's Garland*, no one has yet pretended to guefs. As fome of the fongs have more of the fpirit of poetry than others, it is probably the work of various hands: That it has from time to time been varied and adapted to the phrafe of the times is certain.

In the vifion of PIERCE PLOWMAN, written by ROBERT LONGLAND, a fecular Prieft, and Fellow of Oriel College, and who flourifhed in the reign of Edward III. is this paffage :

> I cannot perfitly my Pater Nofter as the prift it fingeth;
> I can rimes of Robinhod and Randal of Chefter.

DRAYTON in his Poly-Olbion, Song xxvi. thus characterifes him :

> From wealthy abbots' chefts, and churches' abundant ftore,
> What often times he took he fhared amongft the poor :
> No Lordly bifhop came in lufty Robin's way,
> To him before he went but for his pafs muft pay;
> The widow in diftrefs he gracioufly relieved,
> And remedied the wrongs of many a virgin grieved.

HEARNE, in his Gloffary, inferts a manufcript note out of WOOD, containing a paffage cited from JOHN MAJOR, the Scottifh Hiftorian, to this purpofe; that Robin Hood was indeed an arch-robber, but the gentleft thief that ever was : And fays he might have added, from the Harlein MSS. of JOHN FORDUN's Scottifh Chronicle, that he was, though a notorious robber, a man of great charity.

The true name of ROBIN HOOD, was ROBERT FITZ-OOTH, the addition of FITZ, common to many Norman names, was afterwards oftenfomitted or dropped : The two laft letters TH being turn-ed into D, he was called by the common people OOD or HOOD. It is evident he was a man of qua-lity, as by the annexed Pedigree, copied from Dr. STUKELEY's Palæographia Britanniæ : JOHN SCOT, 10th Earl of Huntington, dying *anno* 1237, without iffue R. FITZ-OOTH, was by the female line next heir to that title, as defcended from GILBERT DE GAUNT Earl of Kyme and

Lindfey. The title lying dormant * during the laft
ten years of his life, there could be nothing un-
reafonable or extraordinary in his pretenfions to
that honour. The arms of ROBIN HOOD were
gules, two *bends engrailed or*. In the old garland
he is faid to have been born at Loxley in Stafford-
fhire; and in a fhooting match †, made by the
KING and QUEEN, being chofe by the latter for
her archer, fhe calls him LOXLEY: a cuftom very
common in thofe days to call perfons of eminence
by the name of the town where they were born.

It does not appear that our hero poffeffed an
eftate; perhaps he or his father might be deprived of that on fome political account; attainders
and confifcations being very frequent in thofe
days of Norman tyranny and feudal oppreffion.
In the 19th of HENRY II when the fon of that
king rebelled againft his father, ROBERT DE
FERRERS manned his caftles of Tutbury and
Duffield in behalf of the PRINCE. WILLIAM
FITZ-OOTH, father of our hero, (fuppofe him
connected with the FERRERS, to which his dwelling

---

* The title lay dormant 90 years after ROBERT's death;
namely, till the year 1337, when WILLIAM LORD CLIN-
TON was created Earl of Huntington.

† On this occafion we are told, that ROBIN HOOD was
dreft in fcarlet, and his men in green; and that they all wore
black hats and white feathers.

at Loxley * seems to point) might suffer with them in the consequences of that rebellion, which would not only deprive the family of their estates, but also of their claim to the Earldom of Hunt-ington. From some such cause our hero might be induced to take refuge in those woods and fo-rests, where the bold adventurer,—whether fly-ing from the demands of his injured country, or to avoid the ruthless hand of tyrannic power,—had often found a safe and secure retreat.

Tutbury, and other places in the vicinity of his native town, seems to have been the scene of his juvenile frolics. We afterwards find him at the head of two hundred strong resolute men, and expert archers, ranging the woods and forests of Nottinghamshire, Yorkshire, and other parts of the north of England †.

Charton, in his history of Whitby Abbey, page 146, recites, " That in the days of Abbot " Richard this freebooter, when closely pursued " by the civil or military power, found it neces- " sary to leave his usual haunts, and retreating " cross the moors that surrounded Whitby, " came to the sea coast, where he always had in " readiness some small fishing vessels; and in

---

* The Ferrers were Lords of Loxley.

† Besides many other places, the following are particu-larly mentioned, viz. Barnsdale, Wakefield, Plompton Park, and Fountains-Abbey.

" thefe putting off to fea, he looked upon him-
" felf as quite fecure, and held the whole power
" of the Englifh nation at defiance. The chief
" place of his refort at thefe times, and where his
" boats were generally laid up, was about fix miles
" from Whitby, and is ftill called Robin Hood's
" Bay." Tradition further informs us, that in
one of thefe peregrinations he, attended by his
Lieutenant, JOHN LITTLE, went to dine * with
ABBOT RICHARD, who having heard them often
famed for their great dexterity in fhooting with
the long-bow, begged them after dinner to fhew
him a fpecimen thereof; when to oblige the Abbot, they went up to the top of the Abbey, whence
each of them fhot an arrow, which fell not far
from Whitby Laths, but on the contrary fide of
the lane. In memory of this tranfaction, a pillar
was fet up by the Abbot in the place where each
of the arrows fell, which were ftanding in 1779;
each pillar ftill retaining the name of the owner of
each arrow. Their diftance from Whitby Abbey
is more than a meafured mile, which feems very
far for the flight of an arrow; but when we con-
fider the advantage a fhooter muft have from an
elevation, fo great as the top of the abbey, fituated on a high cliff, the fact will not appear fo very
extraordinary. Thefe very pillars are mentioned,
and the fields called by the aforefaid names in the

---

* Poffibly without invitation.

ld deeds for that ground*, now in the poffeffion of Mr. Thomas Watson. It appears
by his Epitaph, that Robert Fitz-ooth lived
59 years after this time (1188); a very long period
for a life abounding with fo many dangerous en-
erprizes, and rendered obnoxious both to church
and ftate. Perhaps no part of Englifh hiftory
afforded fo fair an opportunity for fuch practices,
is the turbulent reigns of Richard I. King
John, and Henry III.

Hubert, Archbifhop of Canterbury and
chief Jufticiary of England, we are told, iffued
feveral proclamations for the fuppreffing of outlaws; and even fet a price on the head of this
hero. Several ftratagems were ufed to appre-
hend him, but in vain. Force he repelled by
force; nor was he lefs artful than his enemies.
At length being clofely purfued, many of his fol-
owers flain, and the reft difperfed, he took refuge in the Priory of Kirklees, about twelve
miles from Leeds, in Yorkfhire, the Priorefs
at that time being his near relation. Old age,
difappointment, and fatigue, brought on difeafe;
a monk was called in to open a vein, who, either
through ignorance or defign, performed his part
fo ill, that the bleeding could not be ftopped.

---

* That each of the arrows of thefe renowned fhooters fell,
as above defcribed, is probable; but that they were fhot from
fome other place than the top of the Abbey is equally probable.

Believing he fhould not recover, and wifhing to point out the place where his remains might be depofited, he called for his bow and difcharging two arrows, the firft fell in the river Calder, the fecond falling in the park, marked the place of his future fepulture. He died on the 24th of December, in the year 1247 *, as appears by the following epitaph, which was once legible on his tomb, in Kirklees park; where, though the tomb remains, yet the infcription hath been long obliterated. It was, however, preferved by Dr. GALE, Dean of York, and inferted from his papers by Mr. THORESBY, in his Ducat. Leod. and is as follows:

HEAR, UNDERNEAD DIS LATIL STEAN,
LAIZ ROBERT EARL of HUNTINGTON;
NEA ARCIR VER AZ HIE SA GEUD,
AN PIPL KAULD IM ROBIN HEUD:
SICK UTLAWZ AZ HI AN IZ MEN,
VIL ENGLAND NIVR SI AGEN.
    Obit 24 Kal. Dekembris, 1247.

In a fmall grove part of the cemetery formerly belonging to this Priory, is a large flat graveftone, on which is carved the figure of a Crofs de Calvary, extending the whole length of

---

* Suppofing him twenty-one years of age, when on hi vifit to ABBOT RICHARD at Whitby, he muft at this tim have been at leaft in his eightieth year.

ftone, and round the margin is infcribed in Mo-
naftic characters:

+ Dovce : Ihu : de : Nazareh : Donne :
  Mercy : Elizabeh : de . Stanton :
  Priores : de : Cette Maison *.

The lady whofe memory is here recorded, is
faid to have been related to Robin Hood, and
under whofe protection he took refuge fometime
before his death. Thefe being the only monuments, remaining at the place make it probable,
at leaft, that they have been preferved on account
of the fuppofed affinity of the perfons over whofe
remains they were erected.

R. Hood's mother had two fifters †, each older
than herfelf. The firft married Roger Lord
Mowbray ; the other married into the family
of Wake. As neither of thefe could be priorefs of Kirklees, Elizabeth Stanton might
be one of their defcendants.

In the churchyard of Hatherfage, a village in
Derbyfhire, were depofited, as tradition informs

---

* This Norman infcription fhews its antiquity.——
Robin Hood's anceftors were Normans, and poffeffed the
Lordfhip of Kyme, in Lincolnfhire. There is a market-
town in that county called Stanton.

          † Dr. Stukeley.

us, the remains of JOHN LITTLE, the fervant and companion of ROBIN HOOD. The grave is diftinguifhed by a large ftone, placed at the head, and another at the feet; on each of which are yet fome remains of the letters I. L.

═ ∽ ═

THE revolution which delivered the Swifs Cantons from the Germanic yoke, happened about the year 1307. In which WILLIAM TELL, a renowned Archer and inhabitant of Underwald, was the principal inftrument.

GRISLER, the Governor under ALBERT, the Emperor, exercifed the moft glaring acts of tyranny and oppreffion. Amongft the reft of his experiments to try the patience of the people, it is faid that he placed his hat on the top of a pole, and commanded every one to pay the fame refpect to this infignia in his abfence, they did to his perfon when prefent, on pain of fuch punifhment as he fhould think proper to inflict.

WILLIAM TELL refufing this bafe fubmiffion, was brought before GRISER, who knowing him to be a good markfman, wantonly ordered him to fhoot an arrow at an apple placed on the head of his own fon; at the fame time informing him, that if he miffed the mark, he fhould be hanged on the fpot. His fon, then but a child, was placed at the diftance of one hundred and twenty paces from his father; who drawing the bow, with a trembling hand let fly the arrow, which carried away the apple without touching the boy, amidft the fhouts and acclamations of many thoufands of fpectators. The tyrant perceiving he had another arrow concealed under his cloak, afked him,—For what purpofe? as he was only to have one fhot? To which, he boldly replied, " To " have fhot thee to the heart if I had had the " misfortune to kill my fon."

GRISLER, who had promifed to give him his life on his confeffing the truth, now ordered him to be bound and carried prifoner to a place on the lake of Lucern; but TELL happily efcaping out of the boat, in croffing the lake, retired to the mountains. His fellow-citizens, animated by his fortitude and patriotifm, flew to arms, attacked and vanquifhed GRISLER, who fell by an arrow from the hand of TELL. The confequence was that the affociation for independency took place on the inftant *.

≈≈≈

AMONGST the numerous levies made by ED- WARD II. for the purpofe of invading Scotland, in the year 1314, we find particular mention made of the Northumbrian Archers in HARVEY's life of King ROBERT BRUCE, an Heroic Poem, printed in the year 1768.

* See Stumpff & Sceiweizer Chronica, fol. 1548.

From Humber's ftreams, whofe tumbling waves refound,
And deafen all the adjoining coafts around,
To where the Tweed in fofter windings flows,
Full fifty thoufand quiver'd warriors rofe * :——
A hardy race, who well experienced, knew
To fit the fhaft, and twang the bended yew;
Bred up to danger, and inured to dare
In diftant fight, and aim the feather'd war;
Thefe bands their country's higheft triumphs boaft;
And GLOCESTER and HERTFORD led the hoft.

The country from the Humber to the Tweed, formerly the ancient Deira, was ftill covered with woods and forefts, abounding with vaft quantities of game; a circumftance which would certainly encourage the ufe of the bow.

In the year 1341, the 15th of EDWARD III. Sir JOHN ELLAND of Elland, being High Sheriff of the county of York; and the king then engaged in foreign wars: Three gentlemen who lived in the neighbourhood of Elland, namely, Sir ROBERT BEAUMONT QUARMBY of Quarmby, and LOCKWOOD of Lockwood, having by fome means difpleafed the High Sheriff, he refolved on their utter deftruction. Arming his tenants, he repaired by night to each of their houfes, and cruelly murdered them all.

* Thefe troops with many others, fuffered a total defeat at Bannockburn, in confequence of a difpute amongft the officers before the battle began.

LADY BEAUMONT, with her two sons, fled for protection to Brearton-Hall in Lancashire, the seat of SIR THOMAS BREARTON, her near relation. She was presently followed by the two sons of LOCKWOOD and QUARMBY, accompanied by their relation young LACY of Crumble-bottom. These youths were entertained alternately, at the hospitable mansions of Townley and Brearton-Hall; where, besides the ordinary education, they were instructed in all the manly exercises of the times,—riding, fencing, and particularly shooting in the long bow. Here they continued till the youngest of the party had attained to his fifteenth year; when it was unanimously agreed, they should with a few trusty associates return into Yorkshire, and retaliate on the House of Elland, the cruel treatment their families had experienced.

Having prepared every thing for their departure, they set out and travelled through unfrequented paths till they came to Crumble-bottom wood; it being pre-concerted to lay in ambush there, and surprise SIR JOHN ELLAND, coming from the Sheriffturn at Brigg-house. This plan was carried into execution, by openly charging him with his former crimes, and attacking him, surrounded by his servants and retainers. A sharp conflict ensued, in which SIR JOHN being seperated from his friends, was surrounded and slain.

From hence thefe daring adventurers fled to the wildernefs of Fournefs-Fells in Lancafhire; in this place fo remote from fociety and deftitute of every accomodation they fpent the winter, planning fchemes for their future attempts on the remains of a family, they wifhed to extirpate from the face of the earth.

The males of which, now only confifted of a fon and grandfon of the deceafed knight. On the eve of Palm-Sunday, they arrived near the place, took poffeffion of Elland mill, under cover of the night. Here they meant to wait the coming of SIR JOHN ELLAND, his fon, and family, and attack them as they paffed over the ftepping ftones of the river in their way to the church. SIR JOHN having the day before heard, that a band of armed ftrangers had been feen in the neighbourhood; was fo much alarmed, that when entreated by his Lady to attend her to church, he concealed his fufpicions, by putting on armour under his cloaths. The confpirators had a full view of the family as they defcended the hill from the houfe to the river. Already had the Knight begun to crofs the water, when the door of the mill opened, and BEAUMONT holding his bow came forward, and with a determined and refolute air drew the arrow to the head, which flying ftruck the Knight on the breaft, and glanced to a diftance. LOCKWOOD at that inftant ftepped

forth and crying out " Coufin, you fhoot wide,"
difcharged his arrow, which meeting with the
fame refiftance was equally ineffectual; here it is
faid, the Knight was feen to fmile juft before a fecond arrow from the bow of LOCKWOOD, enter-
ing his head laid him dead on the fpot; at the
fame time an arrow from fome other of the party
mortally wounded his only fon, who expired foon
after; and with him the male-line of ELLAND
of Elland *.

Having thus accomplifhed their moft fanguine
intentions, the troop began their retreat with all
poffible expedition, meanwhile the inhabitants of
Elland hearing of the death of their Lord, haftily
collected fuch arms as they could, and came up
with the fugitives in Aneley wood. The loud
fhouts of the people gave notice of their approach;
BEAUMONT, LOCKWOOD, and QUARMBY, had
juft time to face about and form their little corps,
when the enemy appeared in fight. So long as
any arrows remained amongft them this refolute
band did great execution, and flew many of the
Ellanders; but thofe being expended they were
foon overpowered by numbers, and totally defeated. QUARMBY, left wounded in the wood,

* SIR JOHN ELLAND left one only fifter, who carried the
eftate of Elland Hall and the Manor of Elland into the
noble family of SAVILE, by marrying an anceftor of the
late Lord Marquis of Halifax.

was killed by the purfuers. BEAUMONT efcaped to the Continent, ferved under the knights of ST. JOHN in Hungary, and afterwards in the Ifland of Rhodes, with great reputation *. LOCKWOOD after efcaping from his purfuers, arrived at Ca-mel-Hall nigh Cawthorn in the county of York. This houfe was then the property of BOSWELL, the under-fheriff, and tenanted by a perfon of the name of LACY.

LOCKWOOD's ftay here feems to have been pro-longed by an affair of gallantry, which took place betwixt him and the daughter of his hoft. Bos-WELL hearing of this prevailed with LACY to de-liver the unfufpecting LOCKWOOD into his hands; for this purpofe he befet the houfe, and called aloud to the youth to furrender himfelf—who, far from fubmitting, appeared with his bow in his hand, with which he defended himfelf fo well that the fheriff would probably have drawn off his men, had it not been for the perfidy of the daughter of LACY, who rufhing fuddenly upon him cut his bow-ftring afunder, and fled in an inftant. Dif-appointed but not conquered, this intrepid youth ftill refufed to furrender; BOSWELL had then re-

* This gentleman wrote fome years after to one of his friends in Yorkfhire, giving an account of his proceedings abroad. The letter was directed " To JENKIN DIXON, " dwelling at Hole-Houfe, within the parifh Aldmonbury " in the county of York."

courfe to feigned fpeeches, and hypocritical promifes, which fucceeded to his wifh, and the brave
and gallant Lockwood, furrendered himfelf into
the hands of villains, who firft bound him, and
then put him to death. Such were the confe-
quences of this fatal quarrel, which exhibits a
mournful picture of the ferocious manners of the
times *.

=== ∽ ===

Edward III. in the 15th year of his reign
iffued an order to the fheriffs of moft of the Englifh counties; for providing five hundred white
bows and five hundred bundles of arrows for the
then intended war againft France in 1341.

Similar orders were repeated in the following
years; with this difference only, that the fheriff
of Gloucefterfhire is directed to furnifh five hundred painted bows, as well as the fame number of
white. The famous battle of Creffey was fought
four years afterwards, in which the Englifh are
faid to have had four thoufand Archers, who
were oppofed to 15000 Genoefe crofs-bow men.
Thefe having their bow ftrings moiftened with
rain, their arrows fell fhort for want of the ufual
elafticity; the Englifh having guarded againft this
inconvenience, gained a complete victory in 1346.

* Vide Hift. of Halifax.

The battle of Poictiers was fought ten years after, (A. D. 1356) and gained by the superiority of the English Archers.

A. D. 1392, an act passed to oblige servants to shoot with bows and arrows on Holydays and Sundays.

Sometimes the archers gained great victories without the least assistance from the men at arms; particularly the decisive victory over the Scots at Hamildon in 1402. In that bloody battle the men at arms did not strike a stroke; but were mere spectators of the valour and victory of the Archers. The EARL of DOUGLAS who commanded the Scots army in that action, enraged to see his men falling thick around him by showers of arrows, and trusting to the goodness of his armour (which had been three years in making;) accompanied by about eighty lords, knights, and gentlemen in complete armour, rushed forward and attacked the English Archers sword in hand. But he soon had reason to repent his rashness. The English arrows were so sharp and strong, and discharged with so much force, that no armour could repel them. EARL DOUGLAS, after having received five wounds was made prisoner; and all his brave companions were either killed or taken *.

* HENRY's Hist. vol. v. page 463.

PHILIP DE COMINES acknowledges what our own writers affert, that the Englifh Archers excelled thofe of every other nation :

And SIR JOHN FORTESCUE fays again and again, " that the might of the realme of Eng-" land ftandyth upon Archers."

≡ ⌁ ≡

IN 1403 was the battle of Shrewfbury, the beft fought, and the moft defperate that England had ever feen : The Archers on both fides did terrible execution. And here the PRINCE OF WALES, afterwards HENRY V. was wounded in the face by an arrow.

The French depended chiefly on their men at arms, and the Scots on their pikemen ; but the ranks of both were often thinned and thrown into diforder, by flights of arrows, before they could reach their enemies. Of this there are numberlefs inftances, and none where it is more evident than in the battle of Agincourt : Some of the particulars of which, though well known, may not be unacceptable to fome of our readers.

On the morning of Friday, the memorable 25th of October, A. D. 1415, the Englifh and French armies were ranged in order of battle, each in three lines, with bodies of cavalry on each wing.

I

The CONSTABLE D'ALBERT, who commanded the French army, fell into the fnare that was laid for him, by drawing up his army in the plain between two woods. This deprived him in a great meafure of the advantage he fhould have derived from the prodigious fuperiority of his numbers [*] ; obliged him to make his lines unneceffarily deep, about thirty men in file ; to crowd his troops, particularly his cavalry, fo clofe together, that they could hardly move or ufe their arms ; and, in a word, was the chief caufe of all the difafters that followed.

The firft line of the French army, which confifted of eighty thoufand men-at-arms on foot, mixed with four thoufand Archers, and five hundred men at-arms, mounted on each wing, was commanded by the CONSTABLE D'ALBERT, the DUKES of ORLEANS and BOURBON, and many other nobles ; the DUKES of ALENÇON, BRABANT, BAR, &c. conducted the fecond line ; and the EARLS of MARLE, DAMARTINE, FAUCONBERG, &c. were at the head of the third line. The King of England employed various arts to fupply his defect of numbers. He placed two hundred of his beft Archers in am-

---

[*] The Englifh army confifted of about ten thoufand, of whom not a few were fick. That of the French amounted to one hundred thoufand ; fome contemporary writers fay one hundred and forty thoufand.

bufh, in a low meadow, on the flank of the firft line of the French. His own firft line confifted wholly of Archers, four in file; each of whom, befides his bow and arrows, had a battle-ax, a fword, and a ftake pointed with iron at both ends, which he fixed before him in the ground, the point inclining outwards, to protect him from cavalry; which was a new invention, and had a happy effect.

That he might not be encumbered, he difmiffed all his prifoners on their word of honour to fur-render themfelves at Calais, if he obtained the victory,—and lodged all his baggage in the village of Agincourt, in his rear, under a flender guard. The command of the firft line was, at his earneft requeft, committed to EDWARD Duke of York, affifted by the LORDS BEAUMONT, WILLOUGH-BY, and FANHOPE; the fecond was conducted by the KING, with his youngeft brother HUM-PHRY DUKE of GLOUCESTER, the EARLS of OXFORD, MARSHAL, and SUFFOLK; and the third was led by the DUKE of EXETER, the King's uncle.

The lines being formed, the king, in fhining armour, with a crown of gold, adorned with pre-cious ftones, on his helmet, mounted on a fine white horfe, rode along them, and addreffed each corps with a cheerful countenance and ani-

D

mating speeches. To inflame their resentment against their enemies, he told them, that the French had determined to cut off three fingers of the right-hand of every prisoner; and, to rouse their love of honour, he declared, that every soldier in that army who behaved well, should from thenceforth be deemed a gentleman, and entitled to bear coat-armour.

When the two armies were drawn up in this manner, they stood a considerable time gazing at one another in solemn silence. But the King dreading that the French would discover the danger of their situation and decline a battle, commanded the charge to be sounded about ten o'clock in the forenoon. At that instant the first line of the English kneeled down and kissed the ground; and then starting up, discharged a flight of arrows, which did great execution among the crowded ranks of the French. Immediately after, upon a signal being given, the Archers in ambush arose, and discharged their arrows on the flank of the French line, and threw it into some disorder The battle now became general, and raged with uncommon fury. The English Archers having expended all their arrows, threw away their bows, and rushing forward, made dreadful havoc with their swords and battle-axes. The first line of the enemy was, by these means, defeated; its leaders being either killed or taken prisoners.

The second line commanded by the DUKE D'ALENÇON, (who had made a vow to kill or take the King of England, or to perish in the attempt) now advanced to the charge, and was encountered by the second line of the English, conducted by the KING. This conflict was more close and furious than the former—The DUKE of GLOUCESTER, wounded and unhorsed, was protected by his royal brother till he was carried off the field—The DUKE D'ALENÇON forced his way to the KING, and assaulted him with great fury; but that prince brought him to the ground, where he was instantly despatched. Discouraged by this disaster, the second line made no more resistance, and the third fled without striking a blow; yielding a complete and glorious victory to the English, after a violent struggle of three hours duration.

The King, after returning to England, sensible of the very great use and importance of his Archers, directs the sheriffs of counties to collect six wing-feathers from every goose, for the purpose of improving arrows; which were to be paid for by the King. It appears that these six feathers should consist of the second, third, and fourth of each wing.

D 2

JAMES I. of Scotland, who had seen and ad-
mired the dexterity of the English Archers, and
who was himself an excellent Archer, endeavour-
ed to revive the exercise of Archery amongst his
own subjects, by whom it had been too much neglected.   With this view he ridiculed their
aukward manner of handling their bows, in his
humourous Poem of *Christis Kirk of the Grene*[*],
and procured the following law to be made in his
first parliament. (A. D. 1424.)

" That all men might busk them to be
" Archares fra tha be 12 yeres of age, and that
" at ilk tenne punds worth of land there be made
" bow markes, and speciallie near paroche kirks,
" quhair upon halie dayis men may cum and at
" the leift schute thryse about, and have usage
" of Archarie; and whasa usis not Archarie,
" the Laird of the land sall rais of him a wed-
" der; and giff the Laird raisis not the said
" pane, the King's Shiref or his Minisers shall
" rais it to the King."

[*] With that a freynd of his cry'd,—" Fy !"
      And up an arrow drew ;
      He forgit it fae furiously
      The bow in flenderis flew :
      " It was as weel, for if, trow I,"
      For had the tre been trew,
      Men said, that kend his Archery,
      That he had slain enow.

But the untimely death of that excellent **Prince,** which happened in the year 1437, prevented the execution of this law.

≡ ✺ ≡

THE arrow feems to have been the decifive weapon at the great battle of Towton, between the Yorkifts and Lancaftrians, where thirty **fix** thoufand feven hundred and twenty-fix Englifh-**men fell a facrifice to the ambition of contend-**ing Princes.

The battle begun about nine o'clock in the morning of the 29th of March 1461, at which time a thick fnow falling was driven by a **brifk** wind full in the faces of the Lancaftrians, who were thereby prevented from obferving the exact diftance of the enemy.

The LORD FAUCONBERG, an old and ex-perienced officer, **made an** admirable ufe of this accident; for he ordered his men to advance as **near as** they conveniently could, and to difcharge a flight of arrows, and then retire with all fpeed out of the reach of thofe of the enemy.

This ftratagem had a wonderful effect: The Lancaftrians feeling the arrows, and thinking their enemies were not many yards diftant, emp-tied their quivers by repeated difcharges, EDward's men all the while keeping theirs in reserve. The Lord Fauconberg perceiving the Lancastrians' shot was near spent, and that they were advancing, as was customary, sword in hand, to begin a close fight, plied them with another furious discharge, which obliged them to fall back on the main body. Most authors agree, that this conduct of Fauconberg's was a great help to the victory *.

Stow observes that the slain were buried in five great pits in the field by North-Saxton church; and adds, that a Mr. Hungate caused them to be removed from thence, and buried in the churchyard of Saxton; but they were certainly buried in many parts of the field, as their remains are often discovered there by the ploughshare.

Mr. Drake informs us, that in the year 1734, himself and two other gentlemen were present at this place, to see one of these graves opened in the field; where, amongst vast quantities of bones, they found some arrow piles, pieces of broken swords, and five very fresh groat-pieces of Henry IV. V. and VI's. coin. These laying,

---

* Thomas Lord Clifford, noted for his cruelty at the battle of Wakefield, was, three months after, killed at this battle, by a headless arrow, which piercing his throat, he died immediately, aged 26.

nearly altogether, clofe to a thigh bone, made it probable that they had not had time to ftrip the dead before their interment.

=☞=

In the 5th year of EDWARD IV. an act paff-ed, that every Englifhman, and Irifhman dwell-ing with Englifhmen, fhould have an Englifh bow of his own height; which is directed to be made of yew, wych, hazel, afh, or awborne, or any other reafonable tree, according to their power. This act alfo directs, that butts fhall be made in every townfhip, which the inhabitants are obliged to fhoot up and down every feaft day, under the penalty of a halfpenny, when they fhall omit this exercife.

In the 14th year of the fame King it appears, by RYMER's Fœdera, that one thoufand Archers were to be fent to the DUKE of BURGANDY, whofe pay is fettled at fixpence a-day; which is more than a common foldier receives clear in the prefent times, when provifions are much dearer, and the value of money fo much decreafed.

This circumftance feems to prove very clearly, the great eftimation in which Archers were ftill held In the fame year EDWARD, preparing for a war with France, directs the fheriffs to procure bows and arrows, as moft fpecially requifite and neceffary.

RICHARD III. by his attention to Archery, was able to fend one thoufand bow-men to the DUKE of BRETAGNE; and he availed himfelf of the fame troops at the battle of Bofworth: At this battle the Archers, on the fide of KING RICHARD, were commanded by the DUKE of NORFOLK; and the EARL of OXFORD was Captain of thofe of the EARL of RICHMOND.

HENRY VII. directs a large body of Archers to be fent to Brittany, and that they fhall be reviewed before they embark. In the 19th year of his reign, the fame king forbids the ufe of the crofs-bow; " becaufe the long-bow had been " much ufed in this realm, whereby honour and " victory had been gotten againft outward ene- " mies, and the realm greatly defended."

This King inftituted a band of Archers to guard his perfon, under the title of *Yeomen of the Guard*. This band is at prefent eftablifhed; but they are now armed with fwords and halberts, inftead of bows. Still, however, to keep up the memory of their predeceffors fkill, they annually practice fhooting with bows and arrows

HENRY VIII. in the 3d year of his reign, directs, that every father fhould provide a bow

I

and two arrows for his fon, when he fhall be feven years old. Alfo in the 6th of the fame king's reign, every one, except clergy and judges, are obliged to fhoot at butts.

Anno 1510, FERDINAND, King of Arragon, foliciting fuccours from HENRY VIII. againft the Moors in Africa, his defires were complied with, and fifteen hundred Archers fent him under the command of THOMAS LORD DARCY.

Anno 1513, JAMES IV. King of Scotland, invaded the Englifh borders while KING HENRY was in France. The EARL of SURREY, being Lord Lieutenant, raifed the Militia of the northern counties, amounting to twenty-fix thoufand men, and advanced to meet him. The battle (which happened at Flowden Field) was bloody and terminated in the total defeat of the Scots; whofe King, with the Archbifhop of St. Andrews, two Abbots, twelve Earls, and feventeen Lords, were flain in battle. The victory, in a great meafure, feems to have been owing to SIR EDWARD STANLEY and his Archers.

The names of the nobility and gentry who were prefent, with their tenants, at this memorable battle, are recorded in a curious old Poem, faid to have been written by a fchoolmafter at Ingleton, in the Weft Riding of the county of York, which is particularly interefting, as it prefents a striking picture of the manner of raising our ancient Militia, **the** true constitutional force of this country: Men, who **were** one day at the plough, and the next ranged under the banners of their respective leaders with arms in their hands, which they used only against the hostile invader; whom having **repelled, the survivors returned** to their respective employments, amidst the congratulations of their dearest connections, their friends, and their countrymen.

Then might you see on every side *
The ways all fill'd with men of war;
Here silken streamers waving wide,
There polish'd helms glist'ring afar.

From Lancashire and Cheshire fair
They to the lusty STANLEY drew;
From Hornby where as he in haste
Set forward with a comely crew.

What banners brave before him blaz'd,
The people mus'd where he did pass;
Poor husbandmen were much amaz'd,
And women wond'ring, cried,—alas!

Young wives did weep in woeful cheer,
To see their friends in harness drest:
Some rent their clothes, some tore their hair,
Some held their babes unto their breast.

* Henry Jenkins believed he might be about twelve years of age at the time of the battle of Flowden Field, when he was sent to Northallerton with an horse-load of arrows, which a bigger boy had the charge of from thence to the army under the Earl of Surrey.

There woeful mothers mourning flood,
Viewing their fons harnefs'd on horfe:
And fhouting fhriek'd when they forth rode,
And of their lives took little force.

From Penigent to Pendle-hill,
From Linton to Long Addingham,
And all that Craven coafts did till,
They with the lufty CLIFFORD came*.

All Staincliffe hundred went with him,
With ftriplings ftrong from Whorledale,
And all that Hanton hills did climb,
With Longftroth eke and Litton Dale.

Next whom LORD LUMLEY † and LATIMER ‡,
Were equal match'd with all their pow'r;
With whom was next their neighbour near,
LORD CONYERS ftout and ftiff in floure §.

SIR-WALTER AUFITH, fage and grave,
Was with SIR HENRY SHERBURN bent;
And under BULMER's banner brave
The Bifhopric of Durham went ‖.

* Henry, the thirteenth Lord Clifford, on account of the hatred the
Houfe of York bore to his family, was concealed in the difguife of a fhep-
herd, from feven years old till he arrived at his thirty-fecond year ; when,
in the firft parliament of Henry VII. he was reftored in blood and honour,
to all his baronies, lands, and caftles. He died in 1523.

† John Lord Lumley married Joan, fifter to Lord Scroop of Bolton.

‡ John Neville Lord Latimer, married Catherine Par, and leaving her a
widow, fhe became the laft wife of Henry VIII.

§ William Lord Conyers of Hornby Caftle, near Richmond in Yorkfhire, married Maud, daughter of Henry Percy Earl of Northumberland.

‖ There were many ancient families in the North of England at this
time, whofe names are not mentioned in this Poem. But it muft be re-
membered, that the King, with a great part of his nobility, and a numerous army, was then in France.

Whom enfued Sir Christopher Ward,
With him Sir Edward Effingham;
Next went Sir Nicholas Appleyard,
Sir Metham, Sidney, Everingham.

Next went Sir Bold and Butler brave,
Two lufty Knights of Lancafhire;
Then Burkerton bold and Bygot grave,
With Warcup wild, a worthy fquire.

Next Richard Cholmley and Christon ftout,
With men of Hatfield and of Hull;
Laurence of Dun with all his rout,
The people frefh with them did pull.

John Clartice then was 'nexed near
With Stapylton of ftomach ftern;
Next whom Fitz-William forth did fare,
Who martial faites was not to learn.

The next the left-hand wing did wield,
Sir Marmaduke Constable old *;
With him a troop well tried in field,
And eke his fons and kinsfolk bold.

Next him in place was 'nexed near
Lord Scroop † of Bolton ftern and ftout,
On horfeback who had not his peer,
No Englifhman Scots more did doubt.

With him did wend all Wenfadale,
From Morton unto Moifdale Moor;
All they that dwelt on th' Banks of Swale,
With him were bent in harnefs ftour.

* Sir Marmaduke Conftable was High Sheriff of the county of York,
A. D. 1509
† John Lord Scroop married Catherine, daughter of Henry Clifford Earl
of Cumberland.

From Werefdale warlike wights did wend,
From Bifhop's Dale went bow-men bold,—
From Coverdale to Cotter-end,
And all to Kidfton caufey cold ;

From Mollerftang and Middleham,
And all from Mafk and Middleconby,
And all that climb the mountain Cam,
Whofe crown from fnow is feldom free ;

With lufty lads and large of length
Which dwelt at Seimer water-fide,
All Richmondfhire its total ftrength
The lufty Scroup did lead and guide.

Next went Sir Philip Tilney tall,
With him Sir Thomas Barkley brave,
Sir John Radcliffe in arms royal,
And eke Sir William Gascoin grave.

Next whom did pafs with all his rout,
Sir Christopher Pickering proud,
With Sir Bryan Stapylton ftout,
Two valiant knights of noble blood.

Next with Sir John Stanley there yede
The Bishop of Ely's fervants bold,
Sir Lionel Percy eke did lead
Some hundred men well tried and told.

Next went Sir Minham Markinfil *
In armour-coat of cunning work;
The next went Sir John Maundevill,
With him the citizens of York.

* Markenfield of Markenfield nigh Ripon, a knightly family, whofe
only remaining branch is James Markenfield; now inhabiting a fmall
cottage in Stammergate, Ripon, reduced in circumftances, oppreffed with
age, but ftill refpected.

E

Sir George Darcy in banner bright
Did bear a bloody broken fpear,
Next went Sir Magnus with his might,
And Chostance bold of lufty cheer.

Sir Guy Dawnie with his glorious rout,
And then M'Dawbie's fervants bold,
Then Richard Tempest with his rout,
In rere-ward thus their 'ray did hold.

The right-hand wing with all his rout
The lufty Lord Dacres did lead *,
With him the bows of Kendal ftout
With milk-white coats and croffes red.

All Kefwick eke and Cockermouth,
And all from Copeland's craggy hills,
All Weftmoreland both north and fouth,
Whofe weapons were huge maffy bills.

All Carlifle eke and Cumberland,
They with Lord Dacres proud did pafs,
From Branton and from Broughly fands
From Grayftone and from Raven-Glafs.

With ftriplings ftrong from Stanemore fide,
And Auftin-moor men marched kene;
All thofe that Gilfland grave did hide,
With horfemen light from Hefham-Leaven.

All thefe did march in Dacres' band,
All thefe enfued his banner broad;
No luftier Lord was in the land,
Nor more might beaft of birth and blood.

* Thomas Dacre Lord Dacre of Gilfland.

Most lively lads in Lonsdale bred,
With weapons of unweildy weight,
All such as Tatham Fells had fed,
Went under STANLEY's streamer bright.

From Bowland bill-men bold were boun,
With such as Botton banks did hide;
From Wharemore up to Whittington,
And all to Wenning water-side.

From Silverdale to Kent Sand-side,
Whose soil is sown with cockle shells,
From Cartmel eke and Conney side,
With fellows fierce from Furnace Fells.

From Warton unto Warrington,
From Wigan unto Wiresdale,
From Wedicar to Waddington,
From old Ribchester to Ratchdale.

From Poulton and Preston, with pikes,
They with the STANLEY stout forth went,
From Pemberton and Pilling-Dikes
For battle bill-men bold were bent.

Thus STANLEY stout the last of all
Of the rere-ward the rule did wield;
Which done, to Bolton in Glendale,
The total army took the field.

Thus marched forth these men of war,
And every band their banner shew'd,
And trumpets hoarse were heard afar
And glittering harness shining view'd.

E 2

The founding bows were foon up bent,
Some did their arrows fharp up take;
Some did in hand their halberts hent,
Some rufty bills did ruffling fhake.

. . . .

With the rere-ward the river paft,
All ready in ranks and battle array,
They had no need more time to waite,
For victuals they had none that day :

Yet they fuch ftedfaft faith did bear,
Unto their King and native land,
Each one the other did up cheer
Gainft foes to fight whilft they could ftand,

And never flee whilft life did laft,
But rather die by dint of fword.
Thus over plains and hills they pafs'd
Until they came to Sandiford,

A brook of breadth a tailor's yard,
Where th' EARL of SURREY thus did fay,
" Good fellow foldiers, be not fear'd,
" But fight it out like men this day."

Strike but three ftrokes with ftomach ftout,
And fhoot each man fharp arrows three,
And you fha'l fee without all doubt
The beaten Scots begin to flee.

. . . .

The ADMIRAL did plain afpect,
The Scots array'd in battles four :
The man was fage and circumfpect,
And foon perceived that his power

So great a ftrength cou'd not withftand ;
Wherefore he to his father fent,
Defiring him ftraight out of hand
With rere-ward ready to be bent,

And join with him on equal ground :
Whereto the EARL agreed anon ;
Then drum ftruck up with dreadful found,
And trumpets blew with doleful tone.

The ENGLISHMEN their feather'd flights,
Sent out anon from founding bow,
Which wounded many warlike wights,
And many a groom to ground did throw.

On either fide were foldiers flain *,
And ftricken down by ftrength of hand ;
That who cou'd win, none weet might plain, .
The victory in doubt did ftand.

Till at the laft great STANLEY ftout,
Came marching up the mountain fteep,
His folks cou'd hardly faft their feet,
But forc'd on hands and feet to creep.

" My Lancafhire moft lively wights,
" And chofen mates of Chefhire ftrong ;
" From founding bow your feather'd flights,
" Let fiercely fly your foes among."

The noife then made the mountains ring,
And STANLEY ftout, they all did cry,
Out went anon the grey goofe wing,
And 'mongft the Scots did flickering fly.

* Sir Bryan Tunftal of Thurland Caftle, a valiant Captain, was flain
in this battle. He was interred in the chancel of Tunftal church, where
his effigy at full length, cut in ftone, is placed recumbent upon his tomb.

The King himself was wounded fore,
An arrow fierce in's forehead light,
That hardly he cou'd fee his foes
The blood fo blemifhed his fight.

Yet like a warrior ftout he faid,
And fiercely did exhort that tide;
His men to be nothing difmay'd,
But battle boldly there to bide.

But what avail'd his valour great,
Or bold device all was but vain;
His captains keen faii'd at his feet,
And ftandard-bearer down was flain.

THE van-guard was led by LORD THOMAS
and SIR EDWARD HOWARD. The centre by
their father LORD SURREY; and the rear by SIR
EDWARD STANLEY*. The LORD DACRES,
with a body of horfe, was to act as a referve on
all occafions. The king of Scots exhorting his
men to behave like foldiers, immediately joined
battle. SIR EDWARD HOWARD for fometime
fuftained a heavy charge, and had nearly been
routed by the fingular valour of the EARLS
cf LENOX and ARGYLE, had not the LORD

---

* Sir Edward Stanley, after his return from this battle, began to build
the magnificent Chapel of Hornby in Lancashire; on one par of which is
an eagle cut in ftone, and the following infcription, " Edwardus Stanley,
" Miles Dominis Monteagle, me fieri fecit." He dying before it was per-
fected, the parifh finifhed the body of the chapel, which is of inferior workmanfhip.

DACRES, with the Baftard HERON, brought up the referve, and reftored the fight.

LORD THOMAS HOWARD met with a brave refiftance from the EARLS of CRAUFORD and MONTROSE. The KING and the EARL of SURREY maintained a long and a fharp difpute, till SIR EDWARD STANLEY bringing up his Archers, who let fly their arrows with fuch force and effect, that the Scots troops began to give way by opening their ranks. The KING perceiving the diforder redoubled his efforts, and preffing forward with irrefiftible fury, had well nigh overthrown the Englifh ftandard, when LORD THOMAS HOWARD coming to the affiftance of his father, and being joined by LORD DACRE's horfe, immediately gave a turn to the fortune of the day. The Scottifh monarch, with the flower of his nobility and gentry, threw themfelves into a ring, in which form they did all that valiant men could do to defend themfelves; nor did any one exceed the King in perfonal valour; but being mortally wounded in the forehead with an arrow he fell, and with his life ended this fierce and cruel conflict. The royal corpfe being found the next morning, and acknowledged by feveral of both nations, was conveyed to the Charter-houfe, from thence to Shene, a Monaftry in Surrey; "Where," fays STOWE, "it remain-
"ed for a time, in what order I am not certain;
"but fince the diffolution of the Abbeys in the

" reign of Edward VI. Henry Grey, then
" Duke of Suffolk, keeping houfe there, I have
" been fhewed the fame body, as was affirmed,
" wrapped in lead, thrown into an old wafte
" room, amongft old timber, ftone, lead, and
" other rubbifh." A ftrange monument of hu-
man inftability !

＝◆＝

During the reign of Henry VIII. feveral
ftatutes were made for the promotion of Archery.
The 8th of Elizabeth, chap. 10, regulates
the price of bows * ; and the 13th of the fame
reign, chap. 12, enacts, that " bow-ftaves fhall
" be brought into the realme from the Hanfe-
" towns and the eaftward :" So that Archery ftill
continued to be an object of attention in the le-
giflature.

In a fplendid fhooting match at Windfor, before the King, when the exercife was nearly over,
his Majefty obferving one of his guard, named
Barlow, preparing to fhoot, faid to him, " Beat
" them all, and thou fhalt be Duke of Archers."
Barlow drew his bow, executed the King's command, and received the promifed reward ; being
created Duke of Shoreditch, that being the

---

* Eugh Bows, ... 2s. 3d. each.
Bow ftrings, ... 0 6   per dozen.
Livery arrows, ... 1 10   per fheaf.

place of his refidence.   Several others of the
moft expert markfmen **were** honoured with
titles, as EARL of PANCRIDGE, MARQUIS of
CLERKENWELL, &c.

═══〜═══

The following letter inferted in LODGE's *Illu-
ftrations of Britifh Hiftory*, ferves to fhew what
attention was paid to this article in our armies fo
late as the year 1544.

The Lords of the Council to the Earl of Shrewfbury.

" After our right hearty commendations to
" your LORDSHIP, where thies bearers THOMAS
" SCARDEN, and JOHN STODDAR. the King's
" bowyer and fletcher, do preffently repair into
" thofe parts for the putting in order of the
" bowes and arrows, as wele at Barwick, as other
" places theire; and for theire help have alfo with
" them three other bowyers and five fletchers.
" Your Lordfhip fhall underftand, that we have
" delivered unto them conduct-money, and alfo
" wages for one month, to begin at their arrival,
" after the rate following : That is to fay, the
" faid SCARDEN and STODDAR at XIId. by
" the daye, and every of the faid fletchers and
" bowyers VIIId. by the daye; praying your
" Lordfhip to take order for continuance of
" theire wages after the rate aforefaid, when the
" faid month fhall be expired, for the time of

" their being there accordingly.   And thus fare
" your good Lordſhip right hartely well.

> " From Baynard's Caſtle, the XXIId. day of
>   " January 1544.   Your Lordſhip's aſſured
>   " loving friends.
>
>   " THOMAS WRIOTHESLEY,
>   " THOMAS WESTMINSTER,
>   " CHARLES SUFFOLK,
>   " WILLIAM PAGET."

KING HENRY VIII. and QUEEN CATHE-
RINE, came from Greenwich to Shooter's Hill
one May-Day, where they were received by two
hundred Archers, clad in green, with a Captain
perſonating ROBIN HOOD ; who firſt ſhewed the
King the ſkill of his Archers in ſhooting : after
which the Ladies were conducted into the wood,
and feaſted with veniſon and wine, in arbours and
bowers curiouſly decorated.

ON the 17th of September 1583, the London
Archers to the number of three thouſand, with
each a long-bow and four arrows marched to a
place near Shoreditch, called *Hodgſon's Fields*,
where a tent was pitched for the chief citizens.
Proclamation was made by ſound of trumpet that
every man ſhould ſtand at leaſt forty feet from
each ſide of the butts *.

* Theſe butts were diſtant from each other 148 yards.

This exercife lafted two days; on the evening of the fecond day the victors were led off the field mounted on horfes, and attended by two hundred perfons with each a lighted torch in his hand.

The dreffes of this affembly would, at this day, be thought a little fingular. The Archers were diftinguifhed by green ribbons and fafhes; moft part of the company had hats and jerkins of black velvet, doublets of fatin and taffety; and upwards of nine hundred perfons, each of whom wore a chain of gold.

PRINCE HENRY, fon of JAMES I. at eight years of age, learned to fhoot both with the bow and gun; at the fame time this prince had an officer in his eftablifhment who was ftyled *Bow Bearer*.

CHARLES I. appears from the dedication of a treatife, entitled *The Bowman's Glory*, to have been himfelf an Archer. And, in the eighth year of his reign, he iffued a commiffion to the Chancellor, Lord Mayor, and feveral of the Privy Council, to prevent the fields near London being fo inclofed as to interrupt the neceffary and profitable exercife of fhooting; as alfo to lower the mounds where they prevented the view from one mark to another.

This Prince likewife iffued two proclamations in 1631 and 1633, for the promotion of Archery; the laft of which recommends the ufe of the bow and pike together.

$$= \backsim =$$

On the 21ft of March 1661, four hundred Archers marched with flying colours to Hyde-Park, where feveral of the Archers with crofsbows fhot near twenty fcore yards; and fome of them, to the amazement of the fpectators, hit the mark at that very great diftance : There were likewife three fhowers of whiftling arrows. So fplendid was the appearance, and pleafing the exercife, that three regiments of foot laid down their arms to join the fpectators.

$$= \backsim =$$

John King, of Hipperholm near Halifax, in Yorkfhire, was efteemed the beft Archer of his time in England. He was fent for to the court of Charles I. and won great wagers. Being victor at a great fhooting match at Manchefter, during Cromwell's adminiftration, fome of the gentry caufed him to be carried upon men's fhoulders, crying "A King, a King!" Great numbers of republicans being prefent, were alarmed, and cried out as eagerly, "Treafon, treafon! "A plot, a plot!" He died in January 1675.

In the year 1675, three hundred and fifty Archers, most richly habited, appeared in Moorfields to compliment Sir Robert Viner, then Lord Mayor: From thence they marched through Moorgate, Cripplegate, and through Woodstreet into Cheapside; then they passed by the north-side of St. Paul's, and marched round into Cheapside again, and so to Guildhall; where they waited to receive the King, and the then Lord Mayor. When the king had viewed and passed by the Archers, they marched to Christ-church, where a very noble dinner was given, at the expence of the Lord Mayor. Their standard was guarded by six crofs-bow men; all the officers wore green scarfs, and every bowman a green ribbon.

The principal officers were Sir Robert Peyton, Knight, and Mr. Michael Arnold.

On the 26th of May following, the Archers rendezvoused in the military ground near Bloomsbury, and marched from thence through part of Holborn, Chancery-Lane, Temple-Bar, and the Strand, to White-hall, being six abreast; yet, when the van reached Whitehall, the rear was not passed through Temple-Bar. From Whitehall they passed to Tothill-Fields; here they drew up and were reviewed by the King, who marched along their front several times. He was attended by the Dukes of York and Monmouth, and most of the nobility. The Archers were in num-

F

ber about a thoufand; the fpectators near twenty times that number. During the courfe of the day feveral fhowers of whiftling arrows were dif-charged *, with which the company were exceed-ingly entertained.

═ ◡ ═

CATHERINE of PORTUGAL, (Queen to CHARLES II.) feems to have been much pleafed with the fight of this exercife: For in 1676, by the contributions of SIR EDWARD HUN-GERFORD and others, a filver badge for the Marfhal of the fraternity was made, weighing twenty-five ounces, and reprefenting an Archer drawing the long-bow, with the following infcrip-tion:

REGINÆ CATHERINÆ SAGITTARII.

The fupporters were two bow-men, with the arms of England and Portugal.

═ ◡ ═

On the 14th of July, 1681, the London Archers, to the number of one thoufand, under the com-mand of Mr. EDWARDS and Mr. HENRY WAR-REN, marched to Hampton-Court, to fhoot for feveral pieces of plate, viz. Two filver cups and three dozen of filver fpoons. The target was placed upon a butt erected on purpofe upon the

---

* Thefe arrows are fuppofed to have been ufed by the picquet guards, to give notice to the camp of the enemy's ap-proach during the night.

lawn before the palace. The King was pleased to honour them with his presence on the occasion; staid near two hours, and permitted as many of the Archers as pleased to kiss his hand—A mark of the pleasure he took in viewing their exercise.

≡ ✧ ≡

On Friday, April 21, 1682, the Archers under the command of SIR EDWARD HUNGERFORD, COLONEL M. ARNOLD, LIEUTENANT COLONEL J. MOULD, MAJOR H. WARREN, LIEUTENANT E. DONNE, G. WALKER, and J. MANLEY, Captains, met in the artillery ground and marched through Cornhill, Fleetstreet, and the Strand, to Tothill-Fields. The King and most of the nobility honoured them with their company. There were at least one thousand Archers in the field. The recreation lasted for sometime, during which three showers of whistling arrows were discharged. The company, the Archers, and the exercise taken altogether, it was supposed, exceeded any thing of the kind that had hitherto been seen in England.

≡ ✧ ≡

IN Scotland little less attention, though apparently not with equal success, was paid to the encouragement of this art. In both kingdoms it was provided that the importers of merchandise should be obliged, along with their articles of commerce, to import a certain proportion of bows,

F 2

bow-ftaves, and fhafts for arrows. In both every
perfon was enjoined to hold himfelf provided
in bows and arrows : and was prefcribed the
frequent ufe of Archery.   In both a reftraint was
impofed upon the exercife of other games and
fports, left they fhould interfere with the ufe of
the bow ; for it was intended that people fhould
be made expert in the ufe of it as a military weapon, by habituating them to the familiar exercife
of it as an inftrument of amufement.

As there was no material difference between
the activity and bodily ftrength of the two people,
it might be fuppofed that the Eng'ifh and Scots
wielded the bow with an equal vigour and dexterity : But from undoubted hiftorical monuments
it appears, that the former had the fuperiority.
The Englifh fhot with a very long bow. Thofe
who were arrived at their full growth and maturi-
ty, being prohibited from fhooting at any mark
that was not diftant upwards of two hundred and
twenty yards. In the ufe of the bow great dexterity, as well as ftrength, feems to have been requifite. Though we hear of arrows at Cheviot
Chafe which were a yard long; yet it is by no
means to be fuppofed, that the whole band made
ufe of fuch, or could draw them to the head.

The regulation of the Statute of EDWARD IV.
viz. " That the bow fhall not exceed the height
" of a man," is allowed by Archers to have been

well confidered; and as the arrow fhould be half
the length of the bow, this would give an arrow
of a yard in length to thofe only who were fix
feet high.   A ftrong man of this fize in the prefent times, cannot eafily draw above twenty-
feven inches, if the bow is of a proper ftrength
to do execution at a confiderable diftance.   At
the fame time it muft be admitted, that as our
anceftors were obliged by fome of the old ftatutes,
to begin fhooting with the long-bow at the age of
feven, they might have acquired a greater flight
in this exercife than their defcendants.

Not many years ago, there was a man named
TOPHAM, who exhited furprifing feats of ftrength,
and who happened to be at a public houfe near
Iflington, to which the Finfbury Archers reforted,
after their exercife.   TOPHAM confidered the
long-bow as a play-thing, only fit for a child;
upon which one of the Archers laid him a bowl
of punch that he could not draw the arrow two
thirds of its length.   TOPHAM accepted the pro-
pofal with the greateft confidence; but bringing
the arrow to his breaft inftead of his ear, he was
greatly mortified by paying the wager, after many
fruitlefs efforts.

As to the diftance to which an arrow can be
fhot from a long bow, with the beft elevation of
forty-five degrees, that muft neceffarily depend

F 3

much both upon the strength and flight of the
Archer; but in general the distance was reckoned
from eleven to twelve score yards *.

According to NEAD, an Archer might shoot
six arrows in the time of charging and discharg-
ing one musquet.

Arrows are reckoned by sheaves; a sheaf con-
sisting of twenty-four arrows *. They were carried in a quiver, called also an *arrow-case*, which
served for the magazine. Arrows for immediate
use were carried in the girdle. In ancient times
phials of quicklime, or other combustible matter
for burning houses or ships was fixed on the heads
of arrows, and shot from long-bows. Arrows
with wild-fire, and arrows for fire-works, are
mentioned among the stores at Newhaven and
Berwick, 1st of EDWARD VI.

To protect our Archers from the attacks of
the enemy's horse, they carried long stakes pointed at both ends: These they planted in the earth,
sloping before them. In the first of EDWARD VI.
three hundred and thirty of these stakes were in
the stores of the town of Berwick; there were also
at the same time eight bundles of Archers' stakes
in Pontefract Castle.

* By the 33d of HENRY VIII. no one aged twenty-four,
was to shoot at any mark under eleven score yards.

† GROSE on ancient armour.

THE following defcription of an Archer and his accoutrements is given in a MS. written in the time of QUEEN ELIZABETH.

" Captains and officers fhould be fkilful of that
" moft noble weapon; and to fee that their fol-
" diers, according to their draught and ftrength,
" have good bows, well nocked, well ftringed,
" everie ftring whippe in their nocke, and in
" the myddes rubbed with wax,—brafer and
" fhutting glove,—fome fpare ftrynges trymed
" as aforefaid; every man one fheaf of arrows,
" with a cafe of leather, defenfible againft the
" rayne, and in the fame fower and twentie ar-
" rows; whereof eight of them fhould be lighter
" than the refidue, to gall or aftoyne the enemy
" with the hail-fhot of light arrows, before they
" fhall come within the danger of their harquebufe
" fhot. Let every man have a brigandine or a
" little cote of plate, a fkull or hufkin, a maule
" of lead, of five feet in length, and a pike,
" and the fame hanging by his girdle, with a
" hook and a dagger; being thus furnifhed, teach
" them by mufters to march, fhoote, and retire,
" keeping their faces upon the enemy's. Sumtime
" put them into great numbers, as to battell ap-
" parteyneth, and there ufe them often times
" practifed till they be perfect; for thofe men in
" battell ne fkirmifh cannot be fpared. None
" other weapon maye compare with the fame
" noble weapon.".

THE ancient records of the Royal Company
of Archers in Scotland, having been deſtroyed
by fire, about the beginning of the preſent century, no authentic traces of their inſtitution now
remains.   It is ſaid, that they owe their origin to
the Commiſſioners appointed in the reign of
JAMES I. of Scotland, for enforcing and over-
ſeeing the exerciſe of Archery in different counties.   Theſe Commiſſioners, who were in general
men of rank and power, picking out amongſt the
better ſort of people, under their cognizance, the
moſt expert Archers, formed them into a company, and upon perilous occaſions made a preſent
of their ſervices to the king as his chief body
guards.   In which ſituation they often diſtin-
guiſhed themſelves for their loyalty, their courage,
and ſkill in Archery.   This rank of the King's
principal body-guards, the Royal Company ſtill
claim within ſeven miles of the metropolis of
Scotland.

The Company at preſent conſiſts of about one
thouſand in number ; among whom are moſt of the
Scottiſh nobility of the firſt diſtinction.   A number
of theſe gentlemen meet weekly during the ſum-
mer ſeaſon in Edinburgh, and exerciſe themſelves
in the Meadows, ſhooting at butts or rovers.
In the adjoining ground they have a handſome
building, erected within theſe twelve years, with
ſuitable offices, whither they adjourn after their

exercife, and where they hold their elections, and other meetings relative to the bufinefs of the Society.

The prizes belonging to this company, and which are annually fhot for, are; ift. A Silver Arrow, given by the town of Muffelburgh, which appears to have been fhot for as early as the year 1603. The victor in this, as in other prizes, except the King's prize, has the cuftody of it for a year, and then returns it with a medal appended, on which are engraved any motto and device which the gainer's fancy dictates. 2d. A Silver Arrow, given by the town of Peebles, A. D. 1626. 3d. A Silver Arrow, given by the city of Edinburgh, A D. 1709. 4th. A Silver Punch Bowl, of the value of about fifty pounds, made of Scottifh filver, at the expence of the Company, A. D. 1720. 5th. A Piece of Plate, value twenty pounds, called the King's Prize, &c. 1627. This prize becomes the abfolute property of the winner.

All thefe prizes are fhot for at what is termed *rovers*; the marks being placed at the diftance of one hundred and eighty-five yards.

Befides thefe there is another prize annually contended for at butt, or point-blank diftance, called the *Goofe*. The ancient manner of fhooting for this prize was,—a living goofe being built in a turf-butt, with his head only expofed to view; the Archer who firft hit the goofe's head was entitled to the goofe as his reward. But this cuftom, on account of its barbarity, has been long ago laid afide; and in place of the goofe's head, a mark of about an inch diameter, is affixed upon each butt; and the Archer who firft hits this mark is captain of the butt-fhooters for a year.

The affairs of the Company are managed by a Prefes and fix Councellors, who are chofen annually by the whole members. The Council are vefted with the power of receiving or rejecting candidates for admiffion, and of appointing the Company's officers civil and military.

The uniform of the Royal Company of Archers is tartan, lined with white, and trimmed with green and white fringes; a white fafh with green taffels; and a blue bonnet, with a St. Andrew's Crefs and feathers. The Company have two ftandards: The firft of thefe bears on one fide Mars and Cupid encircled in a wreath of thiftles, with this motto, "IN PEACE AND WAR." On the other a eugh tree, with two men dreffed and equipped as Archers, encircled as the former— motto, "DAT GLORIA VIRES."

The other ftandard difplays on one fide a lion rampant, *gules*, on a field *or*, encircled with a wreath; on the top a thiftle and crown,—motto, " NEMO ME IMPUNE LACESSET." On the other, St. Andrew on the crofs, on a field *argent*; at the top a crown,—motto, " DULCE PRO PATRIA PERICULUM."

═ ❧ ═

ROGER ASCHAM, who wrote a treatife on this art in the year 1544, mentions the bracer or leathern guard worn by Archers upon the left arm, to prevent it from being cut by the ftring of the bow. But he recommends fhooting without any bracer, as its ufe may be fuperfeded by giving the bow a greater bend ; that is about nine inches. The fhooting glove was like the bracer, the fame as at prefent. The bow-ftring was made either of filk or hemp.

The bow he recommends to be made out of the bole of a eugh tree, and its ftrength fuch that the Archer could with moderate exertion draw an arrow to the head. The arrow was made of oak or birch, and was of different fizes, according to the different purpofes it was intended for ; its length generally from twenty-feven to.thirty-two inches ; the longeft were ufed in war.

He recommends a goofe's feather for the fhaft, as better than any other. The head of the arrow differed very much from the modern ones. Thofe

2

ufed in fhooting at the marks fomewhat refembling a pine apple, fmooth at top, but furrowed longitudinally.

For war they ufed fharp heads without any barb.

The arrow was always drawn to the ear when they fhot at fhort marks. At long marks or rovers, it was then neceffary on account of the elevation, to be drawn to the breaft.

The Archers did not fhut either eye when they took aim; nor did they look at the arrow, but at the mark only.

BOW-MAKERS.

DURING the laft century, the KELSALS of Manchefter were the beft bow and arrow makers in England; that family is now extinct. The art is revived by JOSEPH WRIGLEY and Co. of Cheetham near Manchefter; who excel all others in the choice of wood, and accuracy of workmanfhip.

Bows and arrows are alfo made and fold by SAMUEL STANWAY near Northwich in Chefhire.

There is alfo a manufactory for implements of Archery eftablifhed by Mr. WARING at Leicefter Houfe.

In ancient times when the demand for thefe articles was univerfal, the bufinefs was divided into separate branches; from whence arose the following Sirnames, viz. BOWYER, BOWER, STRINGER, ARROWSMITH, FLETCHER, &c.

═══✦═══

LANCASHIRE and CHESHIRE ARCHERS.

THESE counties have long been celebrated for their numerous and skilful Archers. About the year 1648, three brothers, JOHN, ROGER, and DANIEL RAWSON, became particularly famous in that science: JAMES the son of JOHN is now (1792) living at Cheetham-Hill near Manchester, aged 76: From the age of eighteen to sixty he never refused a challenge; nor ever lost a match. In the above counties are many societies of bowmen: Few market towns in Lancashire but have one or two sets of butts placed at the several distances of 30, 60, 90, and 120 yards. The Lancashire bowmen hold their meetings at Cheetham-Hill every Wednesday, from Lady-day to Michaelmas, at three in the afternoon. There is also a party, who shoot there every Monday, Wednesday, and Friday, if the weather proves favourable.

MISS BOUVRE, near Warrington, is esteemed the best Archeress in the county. In support of the ancient fame of Lancashire bowmen, LELAND, in his *Collectanea*, hath the following line,

LANCASHERE FAIRE ARCHERE.

G

SCORTON ARCHERS

BEGAN to shoot for a Silver Arrow at Scorton near Richmond, in Yorkshire, May 14, 1673, and have continued ever since.

ARTICLES

Agreed upon by the SOCIETY *of* ARCHERS *at* SCORTON, *May* 14, 1673, *for the regulating of the annual exercise of shooting at the Targets for a Silver Arrow.*

I. IMPRIMIS. THAT every person intending to shoot at this, or other yearly game, for the future, shall deposite and pay into the hands of the Captain and Lieutenant of the Archers (or of some others deputed and appointed by them Stewards to the Company of Archers for that year, the sum of five shillings, or what other sum shall from time to time be concluded and agreed upon by the major part of the Archers; the same to be done some convenient time before the general day of meeting to shoot at the said targets, whereof notice to be publicly given, to the end, that Plate, and such other prizes as are hereafter mentioned, may be had and provided in due time.

II. ITEM. UPON the day appointed for the said exercise, all persons concerned shall repair to the place for the said purpose (to be appointed by the Captain of the Archers for that present year,

which place fhall always be within fix miles of
Eriholme upon Tees, in the county of York,
unlefs otherwife refolved and agreed upon by the
greater number of the Society of Archers prefent
at the fhooting down of the faid targets) by
eight of the clock in the morning ; when and
where a note in writing fhall be taken of thefe intending to fhoot, (the Captain and Lieutenant
excepted) and lots or figures of their numbers
fhall be drawn by fome indifferent perfon ; according to which figures they are to obferve their feveral courfes and orders in fhooting for that time ;
and if any come after the lots are drawn, they
fhall take their places, and fhoot after the laft
figure and according to their coming.

III. ITEM. Two targets fhall be then and
there ready provided by the Captain and Lieutenant, (who hereby are and fhall be exempted
and freed from depofiting any fum or fums of
money, fo long as either of them fhall continue in
their refpective offices) with four circles aptly diftinguifhed with colours ; whereof the innermoft
circle being gilded or yellow, fhall be for the Captain's prize ; and the next to that fhall be for the
Lieutenant's prize ; and the third and fourth, or
outermoft circumferences, fhall be for fuch fpoons
or other prizes of a greater and leffer value, according to the monies depofited, as they fhall be
ordered and proportioned by the Captain and

Lieutenant, and three of the Company of Archers then and there prefent.

IV. ITEM. The faid targets fhall be fet in fome open and plain field, upon two ftraw bafts or mats, breaft-high from the ground, each being diftant from the other at leaft eight fcore yards, at which diftance three rounds fhall be fhot by all the Company, with what manner of fhaft (not exceeding two fhafts) every one pleafeth. The Captain and Lieutenant beginning firft, and then the reft two and two, in order, according to their feveral lots and numbers, till the faid rounds be fhot out at the firft ftand; after which they fhall remove in ten yards, and there fhoot other three rounds in manner aforefaid; and then remove in ten yards more, and fhoot three rounds there; and fo forwards from ftand to ftand, or one removal to another till all the prizes be gotten or fhot down; provided that their faid approach to the targets be never nearer than fixty yards, at which diftance they muft ftand to fhoot them out, if not won before.

V. ITEM. Such perfon as in his due order and place fhall firft pierce or break the Captain's Prize, or any parts thereof with his arrow, (that is to fay) fo as his arrow or any part thereof fhall be within the circle dividing between red and gold, fhall have the filver arrow from the reft, and fhall be efteemed and adjudged Captain of the Archers, and fhall have and enjoy all privileges due and belonging to that office, during the year enfuing; and further fhall have twenty fhillings of fuch monies as fhall be depofited by the Company of Archers at their next annual meeting for fhooting at the targets; when he fhall and muft bring in the faid filver arrow, to be fhot for in manner and form aforefaid. The fame to be done and performed yearly about Whitfuntide, to and by all the fucceffive Captains. Alfo he that in like manner pierceth the Lieutenant's Prize or Circle, fhall have fuch prize or piece of plate as fhall be allotted and appointed by the Captain and Lieutenant for that time. Likewife he that firft pierceth either of the other circumferences fhall have one fpoon (or fuch other prize as fhall be appointed for the fame circle as aforefaid) for every arrow wherewith he fhall pierce or break them, in cafe all the prizes belonging to them be not gotten before. Alfo he that pierceth any of the inner circles in manner aforefaid, whereout the prize or prizes were won before, fhall have one of the beft prizes remaining in the circle, next to that which he fhall fo hit, provided that the fpoons and fuch other prizes as fhall be defigned for the faid two outermoft circles fhall be of two feveral rates and values; and the better of them fhall be allotted and appointed for the circle and circumference next to the Lieutenant's.

G 3

VI. ITEM. If any of the Company shall presume to shoot at the targets out of his due turn of standing, he shall loose his shot for that round (or having shot before) in the next round following : And if any be absent from the stand to shoot in his turn according to his figure, then the next figure there present shall shoot on, that no time may be lost, and shall have such prize as he shall then win. Neverthelefs such absent figure may, at his coming to the place of standing, have liberty to shoot during that round, if the Captain fo pleafe and appoint, either at the time of his coming, or at the end of the fame round, provided that he come before the beginning of the next round.

VII. ITEM. Forasmuch as the Exercise of Archery is lawful, laudable, healthful, and innocent ; and to the end that God's holy name may not be dishonoured by any of that Society, it is agreed and hereby declared, that if any one of them shall that day curse or swear in the hearing of any of the company, and the same be proved before the Captain and Lieutenant, he shall forthwith pay down one shilling, and fo proportionably for every oath; to be distributed by the Captain to the use of the poor of that place or township where they shoot. And in cafe of refusal or neglect to pay the fame, then such party to be excluded from shooting any more till payment is made as aforesaid.

VIII. AND LASTLY. ALL the Company of Archers shall, on the day of shooting at the targets as aforesaid, dine with the Captain and Lieutenant at some ordinary appointed for them near the place of shooting; and if any of them shall refuse or neglect so to do, or not dining with them, shall pay one shilling to the Captain or Lieutenant for his ordinary; then the party so offending shall lose and forfeit the privilege of shooting in the round next following after dinner.

NAMES of the CAPTAINS and LIEUTENANTS of the SCORTON ARCHERS,

From 1673 to 1791;

The TIMES when, and PLACES where the SOCIETY met, and the number of SHOOTERS that appeared at each Meeting.

Time when shot for.	Captains.	Lieutenants.	Place and No. of shooters.
1673, May 14.	Henry Calverley, Esq;	William Wheatley,	Scorton, - - 22
1674, June 4.	George Dobson,	George Dobson,	Barton, - - 22
1675, May 20.	Mr. Samuel Birkbeck,	G. Dobson and T. Allenson,	Eriholme, - - 23
1676, May 9.	Thomas Dodsworth, Esq;	Mr. Samuel Birkbeck,	Croft, - - 17
1677, May 10.	Mr. John Dawson,	Mr. Samuel Birkbeck,	Croft, - - 14
1678, Sept. 5.	Leo. Brakenbury,	Mr. Loftus Squire,	Melsonby, - 7
1679, June 11.	John Murton,	Mr. John Dawson,	Melsonby, - 3
1680, June 8.	Thomas Gyll, Gent.	Mr. Loftus Squire,	Melsonby, - 9
1681, May 12.	Nicholas Thompson,	Leo. Brakenbury,	Barton, - 7
1683, June 15.	Thomas Garthorn,	Nicholas Cole, Esq;	Eriholme, - 12
1684, May 13.	Philip Etherington,	Philip Etherington,	Eriholme, - 14
1685, May 12.	Richard Wilkinson,	Richard Marshall,	Eriholme, - 19
1686, June 8.	Mr. Richard Grimston,	John Sadler,	Eriholme, - 22
1687, May 19.	Leo. Brakenbury,	Percival Robinson,	Melsonby, - 18
1688, July 25.	Mr. Richard Grimston,	Philip Etherington,	Melsonby, - 15
1689, July 4.	Leo. Brakenbury,	John Lawson,	Melsonby, - 14

Time when chosen.	Captains.	Lieutenants.	Place and No. of Archers.
1690, June 12.	Leo. Brakenbury, – – –	Nicholas Thompson, – – –	Melfonby, – – 12
1691, June 18.	William Garthorn	John Pilkington, Gent.	Melfonby, – – 15
1692, May 31.	Mr. Reginald Steadman, –	Mr. George Hartley, – –	Darlington, – 15
1693, May 30.	Mr. George Hartley, – –	Mr. George Trotter, – –	Barton, – – 12
1694, May 30.	Mr. George Hartley, – –	Mr. George Trotter, – –	Middleton-Tyas, 14
1695, July 1.	Mr. Marmaduke Hartley,	Leonard Brakenbury, –	Melfonby, – – 12
1696, July 2.	Mr. Marmaduke Hartley,	Mr. Thomas Gyll, – –	Barton, – – – 13
1697, July 29.	William Raine – –	William Raine, – – –	Middleton-Tyas,14
1700, July 2.	Marmaduke Hartley, – –	Thomas Gyll, – – –	Barton, – – 15
1702, Oct. 1.	Robert Eden, Efq; – –	Mr. William Raine, – –	Darlington, – 9
1703, June 4.	Nicholas Thompson, – –	George Harland, – –	Peircebridge, – 11
1704, Aug. 16.	Nicholas Thompson, – –	Leonard Brakenbury, –	Barton, – – 15
1705, Aug. 1.	Nicholas Thompson, – –	Nicholas Thompson, –	Barton, – – 15
1706, Aug. 14.	Mr. Anthony Hammond,	Ralph Lodge, – – –	Barton, – – 11
1707, June 5.	Mr. Christ. Bridgewater,	Mr. Jos. Etherington,	Hartforth, – – 10
1708, Aug. 27.	Mr. Robert Robinson, –	Mr. Richard Wilson, –	Hartforth, – – 17
1709, July 5.	Mr. Edward Horner, –	Nicholas Thompson, –	Richmond, – – 18
1710, June 27.	Richard Hutchinson and } Robert Robinson, –	Thomas Thwaites, – – –	Richmond, – – 11
1711, Aug. 15.	Leonard Brakenbury – –	George Garnet, – – –	Richmond, – – 15

Time when shot for.	Captains.	Lieutenants.	Place and No. of shooters.
1712, Sept. 15.	Mr. HAMMOND, - - -	Mr. THEOBALDS, - - -	Richmond, - - 21
1713, Sept. 16.	Mr. THOMAS THWAITES, -	RICHARD WILSON, - - -	Hartforth, - - 24
1714, Aug. 16.	Mr. JOHN ROBINSON, -	Mr. EDWARD HORNER, -	Richmond, - - 13
1715, July 19.	Mr. LEONARD HARTLEY,	RICHARD WILSON, - - -	- - - - - - 12
1716, Nov. 5.	Mr. JOHN WILKINSON, -	Mr. THOMAS THWAITES, -	Barton, - - - 17
1717, July 18.	REV. JOHN WILKINSON, -	Mr. ROBERT ROBINSON, -	Pearcebridge, - 9
1718, July 22.	Mr. ROBERT ROBINSON, -	Mr. EDWARD BELL, - -	Richmond, - - 17
1719, May 28.	Mr. THOMAS THWAITES, -	Mr. ROBERT ROBINSON, -	Richmond, - - 8
1720, June 30.	CUTHBERT BOUTH, Efq; -	Mr. R. BERT ROBINSON, -	Richmond, - - 12
1721, Sept. 29.	Mr. ROBERT ROBINSON, -	Mr. EDWARD BELL, - -	Richmond, - - 17
1722, Sept. 6.	ACLOM MILBANKE, Efq; -	CUTHBERT ROUTH, Efq; -	Richmond, - - 15
1723, Sept. 6.	Mr. EDWARD BELL, - -	Mr. JAMES WHITE, - -	Black Bull, - - 15
1724, May 28.	ACLOM MILBANKE, Efq; -	Mr. ROBERT ROBINSON, -	Richmond, - - 15
1725, Sept. 9.	Mr. ROBERT ROBINSON, -	Mr. ROBERT ROBINSON, -	Black Bull, - - 8
1726, June 24.	CODRINGTON JOHN PRESSICK,	Mr. JAMES WHITE, - -	Richmond, - - 13
1727, June 9.	ROBERT ROBINSON, - - -	WILLIAM DOBSON, Gent. -	Yarm, - - - - 12
1728, July 15.	Dr. BELL, Captain, - - -	Mr. ROBERT ROBINSON, -	Croft, - - - - 16
1729, July 17.	WILLIAM BROWN, Efq; - -	JAMES COOKE, Efq; - -	Croft, - - - - 19
1730, June 11.	WILLIAM DAVILE, Jun. Efq;	MATTHEW WASS, Efq;	Richmond, - - 15
1731, Sept. 16.	Mr. CALEB REDSHAW, Jun.	Mr. HENRY NICHOLLS, Jun.	Richmond, - - 13

Time when shot for.	Captains.	Lieutenants.	Place and No. of shooters.
1732, July 27.	Mr. James White,	Mr. Thomas Kelly,	Richmond, — 17
1733, May 31.	Mr. Joseph Coates,	William Browne, Esq;	Peircebridge, — 13
1734, June 20.	Mr. Joseph Coates,	Mr. Peter Marley,	Richmond, — 14
1735, June 24.	Mr. Joseph Coates,	Thomas Thwaites,	Richmond, — 13
1736, June 16.	Mr. John Plumb,	Thomas Kelly,	Richmond, — 16
1737, June 16.	Mr. Peter Marley,	Mr. Peter Marley,	Barton, — 20
1738, June 27.	Rev. Mr. Theobalds,	Sir Hugh Smithson, Bart.	Peircebridge, — 24
1739, July 5.	Mr. James White,	Mr. Joseph Coates,	Love-lane, — 17
1740, July 17.	Thomas Kelly,	Mr. Richard Seymour,	Peircebridge, — 10
1741, June 24, 25.	Thomas Kelly,	Thomas Kelly,	Richmond, — 9
1742, Aug. 12.	Mr. Joseph Coates	Mr. Thomas Watson,	Richmond, — 9
1743, Aug. 2.	Mr. Joseph Coates	Rev. Mr. Theobalds,	Richmond, — 11
1744, Aug. 30.	Mr. Richard Seymour,	Mr. John Plumb,	Richmond — 9
1745, Sept. 4.	Sir Hugh Smithson, Bart.	Caleb Redshaw, Esq;	Peircebridge — 11
1746, Aug. 5.	Mr. Joseph Coates,	Mr. John Plumb,	Stanwick, — 18
1747, Aug. 27.	Mr. Richard Robinson,	Mr. Richard Seymour,	Richmond, — 17
1748, Aug 25,26.	Joseph Appleby,	Thomas Kelly,	Richmond, — 12
1749, Aug. 8.	Mr. Isaac Truman,	Hon. Thomas Vane, Esq;	Darnton, — 15
1750, July 25.	John Bower, Esq;	Hon. Thomas Vane, Esq;	Darlington, — 14
1751, Sept. 5, 6.	Mr. Joseph Appleby	Hon. Thomas Vane, Esq;	Darlington, — 16

Time when shot for.	Captains.	Lieutenants.	Place and No. of shooters.
1752, Aug. 27.	JOHN COLLIER, Jun.	Mr. JOHN WRIGHT,	Darlington, - - 12
1753, July 5.	MARK MILBANKE,	Mr. NICHOLSON,	Darlington, - - 13
1754, July 25.	REV. Mr. NICHOLSON,	WILLIAM CHAYTOR, Esq;	Scorton, - - - 19
1755, Aug. 14.	Mr. JONES,	Mr. ROBINSON,	Hurworth, - - 20
1756, June 11.	ROBERT HALL,	ROBERT DAVISON,	Richmond, - 14
1757, July 15.	THOMAS KITCHING,	Mr. THOMAS WATSON,	Darlington, - 15
1757, July 15.	THOMAS KELLY,	GEORGE RICKERBY,	Darlington, - 16
1758, June 13.	JOHN WRIGHT,	JOHN WRIGHT,	Richmond, - 12
1759, June 21.	GEORGE RICKERBY,	ROBERT HALL,	Darlington, - 19
1760, June 25.	GEORGE RICKERBY,	ROBERT HALL,	Love-lane, - - 13
1761, July 7.	GEORGE RICKERBY,	THOMAS WATSON,	Richmond, - 16
1762, June 29.	GEORGE THOMPSON,	RICHARD HODGSON,	Richmond, - - 15
1763, July 12.	ROBERT HALL,	GEORGE RICKERBY,	Richmond, - 15
1764, Oct. 11.	THOMAS KELLY,	THOMAS KELLY,	Darlington, - 14
1765, July 8.	THOMAS WATSON,	THOMAS KELLY,	Ferryhill, - - 20
1766, June 18.	ROBERT HALL,	JOHN GAINFORD,	Darlington, - 16
1767, July 21.	Mr. THOMAS RAINE,	ROBERT JACKSON,	Darlington, - 18
1768, May 24.	Mr. JAMES PORTEES,	Mr. JOHN GAINFORD,	Hurworth, - - 14
1769, July 4.	Mr. JOHN GAINFORD,	Mr. ROBERT HALL,	Darlington, - 7
1770, July 5.	Mr. ROBERT HALL,	Mr. THOMAS WATSON,	Richmond, - - 9

Time when shot for.	Captains.	Lieutenants.	Place and No. of shooters.
1771, July 24.	Mr. John Gainford, - - - -	Mr. George Rickerby, - -	Darlington, - - 8
1772, July 15.	Mr. George Rickerby, - -	Mr. John Gainford, - - -	Richmond, - - 5
	In 1773 and 1774, the Arrow was not shot for, no Gentlemen appearing.		
1775, July 20.	Mr. Thomas Kelly, - -	Mr. Robert Jackson, - -	Richmond, - - 5
1776, July 30.	Mr. Thomas Kelly, - -	Mr. Macfarlan, - - - -	Richmond, - - 6
	In 1777, the Arrow was not shot for, no Gentlemen appearing.		
1778, July 23.	Mr. Thomas Kelly, - - -	Mr. Robert Jackson, - -	Richmond, - - 5
	In 1779 and 1780—Not shot for.		
1781, July 18.	Mr. Robert Hall, - -	James Gordon, Esq; - -	Richmond, - - 14
1782, June 26, 27.	Mr. Robert Hall, - -	Mr. Henry Wilson, - -	Darlington, - 18
1783, July 10.	James Wilson, - - -	Mr. Robert Hall, - -	Darlington, - - 7
1784, June 22.	Mr. Robert Hall, - -	Mr. Robert Hall, - -	Darlington, - - 8
1785, July 5.	Mr. Robert Hall, - -	Mr. Macfarlan, - - -	Darlington, - - 7
1786, Aug. 15.	Mr. Thomas Watson, -	Seymour Hodgson, Esq; -	Darlington, - - 8
1787, June 26.	Mr. Thomas Watson, -	Mr. John Hayton, - -	Darlington, - - 12
1788, June 27.	Mr. Thomas Watson, -	Mr. Macfarlan, - - -	Darlington, - - 9
1789, Aug. 28.	Mr. John Glenton, - -	Mr. Macfarlan, - - -	Richmond, - - 9
1790, Aug. 18.	Mr. Macfarlan, - - -	Mr. Glenton, - - - -	Richmond, - - 9
1791, June 14.	Mr. Michael Bassett, -	Mr. Macfarlan - - - -	Richmond, - - 9

H

FINSBURY ARCHERS,

Inftituted in the year 1753.

THE few gentlemen now remaining of this Society, are incorporated with the Archers' divifion of the Hon. Artillery Company; and were among thofe who attended his Majefty in the proceffion to St. Paul's on the 23d of April, 1789.

—⚬—

WHARFDALE ARCHERS,

Inftituted in the year 1737.

ARTICLES.

WE whofe names are underwritten, do hereby oblige ourfelves to meet every Thurfday, between the hours of three and fix in the afternoon, at Mrs. BENTHAM's in Otley. And it is further agreed, that every Subfcriber who does not attend according to the above obligation, fhall for every fuch default forfeit fixpence; and if he does attend fhall pay fixpence for his club, otherwife fhall be deemed a defaulter. That his name, forfeiture, and day of the month be entered in a book, kept at Mrs. BENTHAM's for that purpofe. That the forfeitures be paid on a day appointed by a majority of the Subfcribers. That if any one denies on that day to pay his forfeiture or forfeitures, as entered in the book, he fhall be profecuted according to law; and his name upon such refusal, shall be struck out from the list of Subscribers. To prevent any disputes which may be occasioned by the difference of clocks and watches, Mrs. BENTHAM's clock only shall be referred to in all cases relating to the hours appointed as above for meeting. Dated the fourth day of August, 1737.

W. VAVASOUR,	B. KNIGHT,
THO. FAWKES,	HEN. MITTON,
HEN. ATKINSON,	JAS. ROBINSON,
AYS. FAWKES,	ANTH. FOSTER,
FR. FAWKES,	R. MUSGRAVE,
JOHN FAWKES,	THOMAS BOOTH,
WM. BULKLEY,	THO. HARRISON.
C. VAVASOUR,	

How long this Society continued to meet is not now known *.

= ᗯ =

RICHMOND ARCHERS,

INSTITUTED within the borough of Richmond in Yorkshire, in the year 1755,— to meet and shoot for a Silver Cup, on Thursday in every week.

* I have been informed that the butts, used by this Society, were placed near Farnley Hall, and but lately demolished.

DARLINGTON ARCHERS,

INSTITUTED March the 25th, 1758,—to shoot for a Silver Medal and Gorget *; on which day the Articles were agreed upon, and signed by the following gentlemen † :

JAMES ALLAN,	GEO. ALLAN,
ISAAC TRUMAN,	H. THOMPSON,
WM MOORE,	J. MARSH,
ROBERT HALL,	JEREMIAH RUDD,
W. HUTCHINSON,	THO. BURREL,
RHD. SCRUTON,	JOS. APPLEBY,
GEO. RIDSDALE,	WM. CHAYTOR,
WM. NORTON, jun.	RA. TUNSTALL,
JOS. MORLEY,	FRA. LOWSON, jun.
THOMAS WATSON,	RD RICHARDSON,
WM. HOLLAN,	RD MEREWETHER,
THO. KITCHING,	JOSEPH DIXON,
RHD. HODGSON,	EDWARD LOWSON,
JOHN YORK,	THO. PIERSE, jun.
PHIL. CARTER,	JOHN PEASE,
WM. AUNGLE,	JOS. NICHOLSON,
JOHN WRIGHT,	HEN. CHAYTOR.
RHD. SHERWOOD,	

* The motto on the Gorget is, "SECUNDUS HOC CONTENTUS ABITO."

† There was afterwards a Silver Cup added as a third prize, on which is engraven, "TERTIUS HOC CONTENTUS."

VALET: HIC. HONOS. ERIT QUOTIE. LETABRIS SAGITTIS.

Instituted
for the
Gentlemen
Archers
of
DARLENGTON
25
March
1753

Seollon & C.o
Aldersgate St

PARITER. ARCUMQUE. SONANTEM. OSTENDIE. ARTEM. PARITER.

Shooters at this meeting were,

ROBERT HALL,	THO. WATSON,
GEORGE ALLAN,	WM. MOORE,
RHD. HODGSON,	W. HUTCHINSON,
JOS. MORLEY,	GEO. RIDSDALE,
RHD. SHERWOOD,	JOHN WRIGHT,
THO. KITCHING,	WM. HOLLAN.

In September following, a Banner was added to the Medal and Gorget. On this Banner, which was of green filk, was embroidered or painted, feveral golden arrows, tied together with a riband, and furrounded by military trophies.

SEPTEMBER 1, 1758.

Shooters at this meeting were,

THO. KITCHING,	M. NICHOLSON,
THO. WATSON,	G. ALLAN,
RHD. HODGSON,	HEN. CHAYTOR,
THO. PIERSE,	WM. CHAYTOR,
JOHN WRIGHT,	ROBERT HALL.
JOS. MORLEY,	

The Medal was won by Mr. ROBERT HALL, and the Gorget and Banner, by Mr. HENRY CHAYTOR.

MAY 11, 1759.

The Medal was won by Mr. THOMAS WATSON. The Gorget and Banner by Mr. ROBERT HALL.

SEPTEMBER 7, 1759.

Shooters at this meeting were,

THO. WATSON,	GEO. ALLAN,
ROBT. HALL,	RHD. HODGSON,
HUM. THOMPSON,	WM. AUNGLE.

Memorandum. The Medal not won this day. The Gorget was won by Mr. THOMAS WATSON, and the meeting adjourned to one o'clock the next day.

SEPTEMBER 8, 1759.

Shooters at this meeting were,

THO. WATSON,	RHD. HODGSON,
ROBERT HALL,	HUM. THOMPSON,
GEORGE ALLAN,	W. AUNGLE.

The Medal was won by Mr. ROBERT HALL. The Gorget by Mr. THOMAS WATSON.

MAY 13, 1760.

Shooters this day were,

ROBT. HALL,	THO. KITCHING,
THO. WATSON,	WM. HALL.
RHD. HODGSON,	

The Medal was won by Mr. RICHARD HODGSON. The Gorget and Banner by Mr. THOMAS WATSON.

SEPTEMBER 5, 1760.

The Medal was won by Mr. ROBERT HALL. The Gorget by Mr. THOMAS WATSON.

MAY 14, 1761.

The Medal was won by Mr. THOMAS HALL. The Gorget was not shot for.

SEPTEMBER 11, 1761.

The Medal was won by Mr. ROBERT HALL. The Gorget by Mr. RICHARD HODGSON.

AYCLYFFE ARCHERS.

THIS Society met at Ayclyffe, in the county of Durham, May the 24th, 1758, to shoot for a Silver Cup; but continued a very short time.

TOXOPHILITES.

THIS Society was formed by SIR ASHTON LEVER and Mr. WARING. For sometime they shot with few members; but with unwearied attention they have now increased their numbers to one hundred and fifty. They are patronised by his Royal Highness the PRINCE OF WALES, and their President is the DUKE OF NORFOLK.

WOODMEN of ARDEN.

They practice under the patronage of the EARL of AYLESFORD, in Warwickshire.

≡ ↄ ≡

ROYAL BRITISH BOWMEN,

Patronised by his Royal Highness the PRINCE of WALES. They were encouraged and supported by the late SIR WATKIN WILLIAMS WYNNE, his Lady, and most of the first families in the principality. A company of ladies join this Society, who are most expert in the exercise; as is proved by the excellent shooting of LADY CUNLIFF in particular.

The candidates for this Society are ballotted for.—Six black balls exclude.—The subscription is only one guinea *per annum*. By way of practice, detachments meet weekly; but the grand-field day is once a fortnight, at each member's house in rotation. A collation is served under the Society's tent, a limitation is made as to the number of dishes; and the display of any thing *hot* is punished by a fine of five guineas.

A Gold and Silver Medal, with Druidical embellishments, are shot for each field-day. The gentlemen shoot at ninety, the ladies at only sixty yards distance. The uniform for the men is a green coat, white waistcoat and breeches, decorated with the Prince of Wales's plume buttons; the ladies' drefs is white muflin and green ribbons.

≈≈≈

ROYAL KENTISH BOWMEN,

Patronifed alfo by the PRINCE of WALES. They have a moft fuperb and elegant lodge, with a delightful fhooting ground, at Dartford Heath in Kent.

≈≈≈

ROBIN HOOD's BOWMEN.

A fet of Gentlemen who meet near Highgate, and are much increafed of late years.

≈≈≈

LOYAL ARCHERS.

FORMED on the 23d of April, 1789, the day of the general thankfgiving for the reftoration of the King's health —They meet at Lewifham, where their lodge and fhooting ground are pleafantly fituated in a retired and rural fpot.

≈≈≈

THE HAINAULT FORESTERS.

THEY meet under the venerable Oak *, in the foreft of that name in Effex. This Society

* The LORD WARDEN's Records mention a Fair being held under this Oak for near two centuries back ; and there are perfons yet living (1792) who remember the fhade of this wonderful tree covering a ftatute acre of ground. The middle of the ftem is forty feet in circumference.

confifts of ladies, as well as gentlemen, and are compofed of the firft families of the neighbourhood.

$$= \infty =$$

YORKSHIRE ARCHERS.

THIS Society was firft formed in the Summer of the year 1789,—of whom it may be truly faid, both with regard to their dexterity and refpectability, that they are inferior to none.

They fhot their firft Target, May 3, 1790, at Chapel-Town near Leeds, at which meeting,

CARR IBBETSON, Efq; . . Capt. of the target.
JOHN DIXON, Efq; . . . . Capt. of numbers.

JUNE 7, 1790,

Being the next monthly target, it was fhot at Chapel-Town, by appointment of CARR IBBETSON, Efq; who, winning the Medal of Captain of the target, has, on that account, the appointment of the place where the next monthly meeting fhall be held.

At this meeting

SAMUEL RODBARD, Efq; Capt. of the target.
JOHN DIXON, Efq; . . . . Capt. of numbers.

JULY 5, 1790.

This target was fhot at Chapel-Town.

HENRY DIXON, Efq; . . . Capt. of the target.
JOHN DIXON, Efq; . . . . . Capt. of numbers.

AUGUST 2, 1790.

This target was shot at the Granby, Harrogate.

THOMAS FENTON, Esq; . Capt. of the target.
JOHN DIXON, Esq; . . . . . Capt. of numbers.

SEPTEMBER 6, 1790.

This target was shot at Chapel-Town.

WILLIAM LEE, Esq; . . . Capt. of the target.
JOHN DIXON, Esq; . . . . Capt. of numbers.

OCTOBER 4, 1790.

. This target was shot at Ferrybridge.

THOMAS FENTON, Esq; . Capt. of the target.
HENRY DIXON, Esq; . . . Capt. of numbers.

MAY 2, 1791.

This target was shot at Chapel-Town.

SAMUEL RODBARD, Esq; Capt. of the target.
JOHN DIXON, Esq; . . . . . Capt. of numbers.
THOMAS JAQUES, Esq; . . Lieut. of the target.
SAMUEL RODBARD, Esq; Lieut. of numbers.

JUNE 6, 1791.

This target was shot at Chapel-Town.

THOMAS JAQUES, Esq; . Capt. of the target.
JOHN DIXON, Esq; . . . . . Capt. of numbers.
JOHN HANSON, Esq; . . . . Lieut. of the target.
THOMAS JAQUES, Esq; . . Lieut. of numbers.

JULY 4, 1791.

This target was fhot at Heath, near Wakefield.

THOMAS JAQUES, Efq; .. Capt. of the target.
SAMUEL RODBARD, Efq; Capt. of numbers.
THOMAS WYBERG, Efq; Lieut. of the target.
HENRY DIXON, Efq; ... Lieut. of numbers.

AUGUST 1, 1791.

This target was fhot at the Granby, Harrogate.

THOMAS WYBERG, Efq; Capt. of the target.
JOHN DIXON, Efq; ..... { Capt. of numbers.
{ Lieut. of the target.
SAMUEL RODBARD, Efq; Lieut. of numbers.

SEPTEMBER 5, 1791.

This target was fhot on Knavefmire, near York.

THOMAS FENTON, Efq; Capt. of the target.
JOHN DIXON, Efq; ..... { Capt. of numbers.
{ Lieut. of the target.
HENRY DIXON, Efq; ... Lieut. of numbers.

OCTOBER 3, 1791.

This target was fhot at Heath, near Wakefield.

JOHN DIXON, Efq; ..... Capt. of the target.
HENRY DIXON, Efq; ... { Capt. of numbers.
{ Lieut. of the target.
THOMAS WYBERG, Efq; Lieut. of numbers.

Befides the above monthly meetings, the Yorkfhire Archers had a target at the general meeting

of all the Societies in England, held May 27, 1791, on Blackheath, and were within one arrow of gaining a Medal there fhot for.

Their fhooting uniform, is a plain green frock, and velvet cape of the fame colour, with uniform buttons, white waiftcoat and breeches, round black hat, uniform button and loop, with a white oftrich feather, white ftockings, half boots, or black gaiters.—The drefs uniform depends on the pleafure of the Lady Patronefs.

The targets to be always fhot at on public days, at the diftance of one hundred yards.

The four Medals belonging to the Society to be transferable, and to be fhot for at each of the fix monthly meetings.—The Gold Medal for the Captain of the Target, to be gained by the moft centrical fhot during the day — he large Silver Medal to the Captain of Numbers, for the greateft number of fhots in the targets —The Silver Medal for the fecond beft fhot; and the other Silver Medal for the Lieutenant of Num-bers, having the fecond greateft number of fhots in the targets.

The fum of Four Guineas is given by the So-ciety to be fhot for on each target day, and diftri-buted in the following manner; viz. Each arrow, fhot within the gold or centre circle of the targets,

I

receive two fhillings and fixpence; all arrows in the red or fecond circle, two fhillings ; thofe hitting the inner white or third circle, one fhilling and fixpence ; thofe in the black cr fourth circle, one fhilling, and thofe in the outer white or fifth circle, fixpence.

The Patron of the Society, EARL FITZWILLIAM —The Patronefs, the COUNTESS of MEXBOROUGH.

The Society confifts at prefent of feventy-four members, with four honorary ones.

'The Ladies prefented the Society laft fummer, with very elegant Colours, to be placed on the top of a large Tent belonging the Society, in which a company of eighty may with great convenience dine.

=⟡=

THE MERCIAN BOWMEN,

A very refpectable Society, who meet on Summer Hill, near Coventry.

=⟡=

THE KENTISH RANGERS.

A Society who meet on Blackheath, and are formed of members who have feparated from one of the cther Societies.

SOUTHAMPTON ARCHERS,

Now Royal, being patronifed by his Royal Highnefs the DUKE of GLOUCESTER.

BOWMEN OF CHEVY-CHACE,

Under the immediate patronage of the DUKE of NORTHUMBERLAND.

WOODMEN OF HORNSEY.

SURREY BOWMEN,

Who are alfo become Royal, having his Royal Highnefs the DUKE of CLARENCE as patron. This Society has of late been particularly diftinguifhed, and promifes to vie with any in point of dexterity and fkill.

THE ARCHERS OF ARCHENFIELD,

Near Hereford, have been much fpoken of, both for their dexterity and hofpitality.

I 2

THE grand Annual Meeting of the following Societies of Archers, took place on Friday, the 27th of May, 1791, at Blackheath, viz.

HONOURABLE THE ARTILLERY COMPANY, in two divisions,
SURREY BOWMEN, first division,
——————————— second division,
HAINAULT FORESTERS,
TOXOPHOLITES, first division,
——————— second division,
NORTHUMBERLAND ARCHERS,
SHERWOOD FORESTERS,
KENTISH RANGERS,
KENTISH BOWMEN,
LOYAL ARCHERS,
WOODMEN OF ARDEN,
ROBIN HOOD SOCIETY,
YORKSHIRE ARCHERS,
WOODMEN OF HORNSEY.

They were all dressed in green, with half-boots. Numbers of ladies were likewise dressed in the uniform of the Societies. Thirty-two targets were placed on the ground, and about a dozen of Archers appointed to shoot at each.—At twelve o'clock the shooting for the prizes commenced, and continued without intermission till three; when they retired to their tents, and partook of some refreshments. After which, the contest was renewed; and on examining the targets at six o'clock, Mr. RICKARDS, of the Toxopholite Society, appeared to be entitled to the Gold Medal; and Mr. RUSH of the Woodmen of Hornsey, to the Silver Medal. LORD AYLES-BURY, having shot sixteen different times into the target, he was declared Captain of Numbers. The Archers afterwards returned to town, and dined together at the Thatched-House Tavern.

The Loyal Archers shot once into the Bull's Eye of the Target; the Yorkshire Archers once; the Toxopholite Society twice; the Robin Hood once; and the Woodmen of Hornsey twice.

Two persons were slightly wounded by standing too near the targets.

The tents were fancifully decorated with banners, proudly displaying the devices of the various orders of Archery.

THUS have we seen in the lapse of time, one of the most dangerous and destructive weapons of war laid aside, to make room for a novel invention; and English Archery, once the terror of foreign enemies, now changed into a pleasing, elegant, and healthful amusement. May we not wish for a similar alteration with regard to every other inftrument invented for the deftruction of men; and hope for the arrival of thofe peaceful days, fo beautifully defcribed by the poet——

No more fha'l nation againft nation rife,
Nor ardent warriors meet with hateful eyes;
Nor fields with gleaming fteel be cover'd o'er,
The brazen trumpets kindle rage no more;
But ufelefs lances into fcythes fhall bend,
And the broad falchion in a plowfhare end.

INDEX.

Page.

Page.

T H E   E N D.

www.ingramcontent.com/pod-product-compliance
Lightning Source LLC
Chambersburg PA
CBHW032148010726
47493CB00008BA/2632